A

HOUSE

OF

RUIN

A

HOUSE

OF

RUIN

The Story Behind the Execution Estate

A Slow Ruin Companion Story

PAMELA CRANE

Tabella House
Raleigh, North Carolina

Thank you for supporting authors and literacy by purchasing this book. Want to add more gripping reads to your library? As the author of more than a dozen award-winning and bestselling books, you can find all of Pamela Crane's works on her website at www.pamelacrane.com.

To my fans who have supported me in ways I will never forget. This was written especially for you.

Author's Note

If you've read *A Slow Ruin* (it's the book with my daughter's picture on the cover—go grab a copy if you haven't yet!), you're familiar with the Portman family who live in a gorgeous Victorian mansion nestled in Oakmont, Pennsylvania (loosely based on a real house that I had the joy of researching). What's better than a stately old mansion? A mansion steeped in murder and mystery! Thus, the Execution Estate was born.

In *A Slow Ruin*, the book mentions a 1982 murder that happened in the library—perpetrated by Professor Plum with the candlestick...kidding! It's not that story, rather it's one where a family of five was brutally murdered one bitter November night. The massacre was so horrific that the home was forever branded the "Execution Estate," for something about that house destroyed everyone who lived there, from the family that first occupied it to the last. Some say it was coincidence. Others say it was a curse.

Well, that 1982 murder was never solved (I can only blame myself as the writer). But now you're about to uncover what happened on that fateful night all those years ago that left a family of five slayed in their library (because...where else?). Was it with the candlestick? At the hands of a brooding butler? Without giving away the killer or the weapon just yet, all I can tell you is that it was a murder that left investigators stumped as the case grew colder and colder every year (cue suspenseful music: dun dun duuuun).

Why did I feel the need to tell this story? It was a loose thread I had intended to leave in *A Slow Ruin* because it was a mystery I myself wanted to unravel separately. A family slayed. Six suspects who worked in the house. Each with a dark past and a motive to kill.

Meet Derl Newman, the creaky-boned estate manager who found the victims. He's still alive, and he hasn't been able to forget the night he found the Eyler family not just shot dead, but mutilated. Despite the wealth of information he provided to the police during the initial investigation, they couldn't pin the murder on any of the house staff. They all had motive. They all had alibis. And what a motley crew they are! But Derl's back, and he's telling the world his story this time.

In the upcoming chapters you'll meet a cast inspired by various thriller book and movie characters that I have enjoyed getting to know over the years. Think you can figure some of them out? I dare you to try. Plus, you'll get acquainted with an odd family harboring a lot of sins and secrets.

If you enjoy a fun little whodunit, I hope you'll give this one a shot! (No pun intended…or is there? Mwah ha ha!)

A HOUSE OF RUIN

The Times Tabloid

CAT EATS EVIDENCE IN HOMICIDAL CATASTROPHE

*Pittsburgh, PA
Monday, November 30, 1982*

The cat's out of the bag as a grisly turn of events last week goes public. A murder mystery at a sprawling Oakmont mansion has left police completely baffled.

The famed Eyler family, murdered in their library, was left eyeless in one of the most inexplicable murders of our time. The victims included star sci-fi literary agent Tony Eyler, his philanthropist wife Duchess Jill Eyler, and their three unremarkable children.

After being shot, they were subsequently mutilated as an eye was removed from each victim and a book placed on each of their faces. As of yet, police don't yet have a suspect to throw the book at. Though the butler, with the revolver, are at the top of the list.

As if that wasn't enough, the cat took a turn with the victims, eating bits and pieces of them. Investigators are hoping the feline will cough up a hairball that could contain hair samples from the killer.

Investigators have yet to see eye to eye on possible suspects in this eye-plucking murder. This slaying will certainly go down in the books…though not the sci-fi genre Tony is famous for.

Prologue

November 26, 1982

It was a weekly tradition, the family nestled in a semicircle around the library's hearth while the father read aloud, a tradition that would end in their deaths. While the steady beat of Tony Eyler's words drummed against the massive space, warmed by a crackling fire, the children were too enthralled to hear the approaching footsteps outside the door.

The mother was too preoccupied with a tricky crochet stitch to notice the creak of hinges opening.

The father was too focused on the story he was reading to feel the presence of an uninvited guest.

The cat was too disinterested to care about the figure unlocking the glass case that secured the 9mm pistol.

The house was too secluded for the neighbors to detect the gunshots that pierced the silent night.

Only the slightest creak from a loose floorboard alerted Tony Eyler that someone else was in the library. Glancing up, his gaze locked on his assailant, then slowly navigated down to the gun in hand. A gasp escaped his mouth as realization hit him…along with the first bullet.

The projectile zipped across the room, instantly embedding itself in Tony's chest. The book he was holding smacked to the floor; his body slumped in the plush armchair now soaked in his blood.

The unwavering hand that held the gun next aimed for the mother. While Jill scrambled to collect her children to safety, their screams joined in the thunder of a second bullet splitting her chest open. She dropped instantly to the hardwood, her last moments a whispered plea for the killer to spare her children.

The last three shots were met with tears and begging as one, two, three children were sent to untimely graves. First Charlotte, the oldest, futilely blocking her siblings with outstretched arms. When her body fell with a dull thump, her brother Dustin sobbed behind her, hugging his remaining sister as the next bullet came for him. Last was the youngest, Jennifer, whimpering, tears wetting her cheeks. The shooter hesitated with this one, as if humanity had surfaced for only a moment before cold-blooded hatred prevailed. Then the final gunshot rang out…

If only it had ended there.

But it was just the beginning. For the killer wasn't content to simply end the Eyler bloodline; each member of the family must suffer one final humiliation.

Dragging the bodies across the floor, a smeared

bloody trail in each body's wake, the killer formed the family into a pentagram shape connected by their feet. Once done, the killer plucked the right eyeball from each of the victims using a small knife. It was a gruesome task, but necessary.

An eye for an eye, a tooth for a tooth. It was the price for cruelty. As the Eyler family had taken much, so much would be taken from them. They had been blind to all the pain they had caused to those around them, thus it felt a fitting gesture.

The killer assessed his handiwork, but it wasn't yet complete. One final stroke was needed to paint the perfect picture. Lastly, and most importantly, were the books. First the one Tony had been reading from, a first edition of *The Hobbit,* his most prized possession, was gently splayed open across his mutilated face. The other literary selections were plucked from the vast floor-to-ceiling bookshelves, handpicked for the mother and three children, a title resting open across each horrified one-eyed expression.

Soon the police would arrive on the scene, and investigators would gasp in horror, covering their noses from the putrid reek of decay. Tony Eyler would no longer be remembered for the famous authors he represented, nor Jill for her literary nonprofits she organized, nor the children for simply owning the Eyler name. Today they would go down in infamy as the family brutally murdered in their pretentious mansion, and perhaps, if fate decreed, all their sins would be exposed.

The killer had planned every gory detail, creating a scene so dreadful it was guaranteed the dominate the news. A scene too terrible to ever forget. Too graphic to miss the message. Today this house, celebrated for its dollhouse-like architecture, had been home to the insufferably arrogant Eyler family. Tomorrow it would be branded the *Execution Estate,* a house of horror.

As the killer stood at the fireplace hearth examining the scene, both proud and distraught by his creation, the intended message seeped out from the blood on the floor, the books covering their faces, the holes in their hearts:

Time does not heal all wounds.

Chapter 1

Now

I waited at the library door, a room that could have been magical, if not for the horror that stained the floorboards. As the hinges squeaked, begging for lubricant, I felt the past in this room rise from its grave. A shiver shook my old bones. Not from the bitter autumn chill that seeped through the walls and single-pane glass window overlooking the estate's hibernating grounds, but from the presence of an evil that still lingered here. Even forty years after the murder, I felt it pulsing. Reaching for me. This house would never let me forget.

Trust me, I had tried.

The image crept up on me. Crowded my vision. Five bodies—father, mother, two daughters, and son—like points of a dying star. Bloody blossoms on their clothes, sticky residue across the floor. Faces covered with open books…and rightly so, because what was hidden beneath was too gruesome to put on display.

Help me, a whisper caught on the stale air.

11

No one was here but me.

Help me, I heard again.

No one but me and apparently their lost souls.

"I…I don't know how," I whispered back. My voice cracked with the dry sound of someone who hadn't spoken in decades.

Help me, more urgent this time.

"Please tell me how," I begged. Tears dripped down my cheek in memory of this family I had once cared for. Forty years ago I had the misfortune of finding their bodies; forty years later I still couldn't expunge the ghastly scene from my memory.

Two stories down, I heard a car door slam shut, delivering me from the recurring daymare. I mumbled gratitude for the small mercy. She was here. It was time.

Famed documentarian Keisha Fenty had agreed to meet me in the Oakmont, Pennsylvania, mansion called the *Execution Estate,* thus christened after the brutal killing of the Eyler family that had lived here. Over the years the dwelling had attained a regrettable notoriety, sought after by haunted house enthusiasts and horror-loving looky-loos. Eventually another family, the Portmans, found the courage to overlook its scandalous past and build a life here. I couldn't help but wonder how long the Portmans would survive before the house destroyed them too. As for me, I preferred to stay as far away from it as possible. Unfortunately, my resolve was not as strong as the house's unsavory allure.

After a random letter showed up in my mailbox weeks ago, it took me days to reply. Though my mind often faded these days, the words of the handwritten note stuck in my brain:

Dear Mr. Newman:

It took me a while to track you down and find your mailing address, so I hope this reaches you. I understand you were the estate manager for the Eyler family in 1982, and the one who found their bodies. I've been in touch with the lead investigator on the case, and I was wondering if I might interview you for an unsolved mysteries documentary I'm producing about the Eylers' murder. While I understand you might be reluctant to revisit this tragedy, I hope you'll consider this an opportunity to provide closure for you and the family.

My contact information is below, if you'd allow me to speak with you in person.

Thank you for your time,

Keisha Fenty

The sender was kind, courteous, professional. Reminiscent of how the police investigators had treated me while I was still in shock after discovering five dead bodies in this very spot where I stood.

I glanced down at my classic black pinch penny loafers—some fashions never go out of style—unaware I had somehow drifted to where the blood still stained the floor. Without my knowing, the Eyler family ghosts pulled me here, their siren call drawing me closer. I shuffled back to the doorway to safety, my joints groaning like the ancient floorboards, as a sudden fear swept over me.

Clearly Ms. Fenty didn't understand much about what I had endured. Or what I continued to endure. I was terrified, only wanting to forget. Every arthritic bone in my body warned me to turn down her request. But she offered one thing that time and therapy could not: justice.

During the initial investigation I had voiced my suspicions of who had done it and why. The Eyler estate was teeming with suspects—a bitter butler with an ax to grind, the cagy chef who loathed his job, the gardener with a grudge, the maid hiding her fair share of mischief. Even the mailman had a motive.

I had explained all this to the lead detective, who professed to find my insights invaluable. But without sufficient evidence, and investigative techniques in the 1980s being primitive by today's standards, no immediate arrest was made. I'm afraid I made a pest of myself, over the ensuing months and years, by contacting the detective upon my recollection of the slightest minutiae. As the murders eventually became just another cold case, my voice dwindled to silence. Now was my chance to address the public on a much larger platform.

Agreeing to the interview certainly was a risk, regurgitating the most traumatic memory of my life in front of a camera. And in the very place that birthed my nightmares. But in a way, I'd been preparing for this moment ever since that night. I yearned to end the nightmare as much as the nightmare yearned to end me.

What else could I add that I hadn't already told police? That the aftermath of Friday, November 26, 1982, would forever traumatize me? That I would never again be able to hold a full-time job? That I battled recurring hallucinations of the bodies rising up from their graves, seeking vengeance? After all, the killer had never been found, and had never killed again…as far as the police knew.

Keisha had no idea what she was in for, not really. How could she? After all, she wasn't the one who had walked into this very library on a cold November day to find a husband, wife, and their three children, bellies stuffed from the previous night's Thanksgiving dinner, shot execution style, a book splayed on each of their faces, covering the missing eye that had been ruthlessly gouged out by their killer. It was my curse that the shadow of that grotesque scene should fall upon me all these decades later.

Although every member of the house staff was questioned, every lead tracked down, the police had come up emptyhanded, with neither a motive identified nor or a shred of convicting evidence found. Well, until now, that is.

Which was why I was here, standing at the threshold

where my trauma originated and still resided, waiting to share once again what I knew, and how I had come to discover who killed the Eyler family and why.

I'm no Remington Steele, the lead detective had tactfully informed me way back when—although I appreciated the comparison to the debonair TV detective. But as the years passed and I watched the staff of the Execution Estate go on with their lives—and deaths— while I remained stuck in my living nightmare, eventually the answer would reveal itself to me.

Answers were buried in the little things. A comment that didn't quite fit, like a misshapen puzzle piece. Or a behavior that seemed off. Separately they were idiosyncrasies, but together they were clues. Clues that eventually led me to the aha moment of discovering the killer.

Who killed the Eyler family in their mansion's library that fateful night, you ask?

It's not so simple as a name. First you must understand the graphic details surrounding one of the most horrifying murders of the twentieth century in their full context. And then you must explore the history of the individuals who had something to gain—or something to lose—from the Eyler family's demise.

Downstairs the heavy oak front door slammed shut. I heard the tap of footsteps across the hardwood entryway, then the treads creaking as Miss Fenty climbed the first flight of stairs. She paused on the landing—probably to take in the impressive stained-glass window depicting the Victorian couple that built this monstrosity of a home. Up the next flight the footsteps resumed until they paused somewhere behind me in the shadows of the hallway.

"Mr. Newman?" I recognized her voice from the many phone calls we'd had as plans were arranged, details exchanged, in preparation for today's interview.

"Miss Fenty, I'm in the library!" I called to her.

A *tap-tap-tap* of high heels and Keisha Fenty stood before me. Her dark skin offered a striking contrast against a white wool coat, where mustard yellow cuffs peeked out from each sleeve. When she smiled, her brown eyes sparkled with what I read as rare kindness, especially in this narcissistic age. Chin-length ringlets framed her heart-shaped face. I briefly wondered how someone so beautiful could be fascinated by something so ugly as murder.

While some critics dismissed her unsolved mystery documentaries as tabloid TV garbage, they'd been ratings bonanzas, fueling renewed interest in cold cases and, more often than not, helping to bring the killer to justice. Her subsequent interviews of these twisted murderers were probing and unflinching, even as they revealed lurid details best left to the imagination. Critics still scoffed, but criminal profilers regarded these programs as valuable primers into the psychotic mind.

"It's a pleasure to finally meet you in person," she said, extending her gloved hand. In the other hand she carried a large purse.

"You as well, Miss Fenty." I embraced her hand in mine, self-conscious of the swollen bulbs of my aging knuckles.

"Keisha, please," she corrected me gently. "I feel like we're practically friends, considering how often we've spoken the past few weeks."

"Then I suppose you ought to just call me Derl." I grinned, catching a glimpse of myself in the gilt-framed mirror hanging on the far wall. I was a much younger man, with a full head of hair and a trim body, the last time I'd gazed into this mirror. Now I was a very old man with a balding pate and a paunch. I reflexively sucked in my gut, as if this beautiful young woman would have any interest in an old fossil like me.

Feeling a slight tightness in my chest and neck, I reached up to loosen my tie. I regretted my choice to use a café knot, an extremely complex style of knot that didn't have much give.

"Are you okay?" Keisha asked with concern.

"Yes, of course. Just a little warm in here." My eyes caught the large fabric buttons of her overcoat, and the unique 1950s stitching. "Is that a vintage Peau de Faille overcoat?" I wondered aloud.

She chuckled, clearly impressed. "It sure is. You know your fashion."

"I used to work for a fashion designer before becoming caretaker for the Eylers."

"That's quite a career change."

"Not by choice. When I caught my boss taking advantage of his assistant and reported it to HR, it was either me or him. You can guess who was more integral to the company. But fashion is still a passion of mine, though I'm far too old to know what's trendy anymore."

"Trendy is a state of mind." She gave my arm a gentle squeeze, then skimmed the room from wall to book-covered wall, floor to arched ceiling, where above the beams a lone spire pierced the broody sky.

"Wow, this place is incredible." Her gaze settled back down to me. "How did you convince the family that lives here to let us film on site? They fervently declined when I had asked."

"I guess you could say I have my charm." I took a slight bow. "Though I'm surprised to see it hasn't changed much since I was last here."

"Really? I wonder why. There's got to be thousands of dollars' worth of books in here." She nodded toward the antique gun case on the wall. "And I'm sure someone could have sold the guns for a pretty penny."

"After the Eylers passed, no one wanted to have anything to do with this place. So the estate left everything in the house to be sold with it, including the books and furniture. I guess the Portman family liked it all enough to keep it."

Keisha ran a gloved fingertip along the dirty spine of a book. "Or they haven't bothered to really check it out…"

"Would you, after what happened here?"

"Absolutely! It's the most intriguing room in the house. But … I'm not like most people, I suppose." She wiped the grime off her glove and turned to the center of the library. "Well, Derl, while we wait for my cameraman to arrive, let's sit down and chat for a moment." She led me toward the armchairs around the empty fireplace's hearth.

Her stride showed a confidence I didn't feel, for she was unaware of the true nature of what happened here. Still, I followed her across the room, along a dusty floor-to-ceiling bookcase packed with precious hardcovers, rare signed copies, and some more recent literary collections that had been passed down with the house. Pausing at the gap where the Unwin & Allen first edition of *The Hobbit* should have been, I involuntarily cringed. Mr. Eyler would turn over in his grave if he knew his pride and joy had been propped open across his face, hiding his gaping eye socket.

I bumped into the rolling library ladder, wheels rigid with rust. Keisha jolted at the squeal. "What was that?"

For all of her cool demeaner, even she felt the darkness lurking here.

I pointed to the ladder. "Apologies for my clumsiness, ma'am. Sometimes I swear this house is alive."

"If it was, it'd make my job a whole lot easier." Keisha sat in one chair and gestured to the other one opposite her. While she set down her purse and removed her coat and gloves, a dark memory stalked me.

Standing before the hollow fireplace, I envisioned the bodies that had been strewn here, blood pooling on this very floor. I shook it off and sat with an achy groan, wondering whose flesh had last warmed this seat. The thought taunted me.

"My cameraman should be here any moment," Keisha said as she peered around me at the open door, "but I wanted to make sure you were comfortable before we began. And also answer any questions you have."

I shrugged. "Everything seems pretty straightforward, far as I'm concerned. You ask questions, I answer. Then you put it all together and hopefully make the police finally believe me."

"It sounds like you've been thinking about this murder for a while."

My inflamed joints radiated pain. I cracked a knuckle, relishing the pop of relief before I answered. "Sure have. Not much else to do but dwell on it."

"I can relate. This case is of particular interest to me, mainly because no one else has been able to figure it out. I guess you could say I like the challenge."

After pulling an envelope from her purse, Keisha leaned toward me, handing me a large crime scene photograph. The image instantly dragged me back to that night—when I first saw Tony Eyler's dead body. This color photo captured that horrible moment in agonizing detail.

Keisha, seeing the repulsion on my face, instantly grabbed it back. "I'm so sorry. I shouldn't have shown you that."

I shook my head, willing the swelling nausea back down. "No, it's okay. It's just…difficult…seeing it again."

She placed the photograph upside down on her lap just as the cameraman, a chubby, bearded fellow in a porkpie hat, tramped into the room. He sported an unbuttoned Hawaiian shirt over a dingy, wrinkled T-shirt that he must have been wearing for days. His cutoff denim shorts left frighteningly little to the imagination. It appalls me how the younger generation thinks it's acceptable to go around looking like an unmade bed. He gave me a curt chin jerk fashionable with the too-cool-to-say-hello crowd and went about setting up his equipment. Keisha didn't bother to introduce him. One look at him was all the introduction I needed.

Grabbing a notebook and pen, Keisha returned her attention to me. "Before we begin, in one of our calls you mentioned you knew a lot about the Eyler family secrets. Care to tell me who your source is?"

"I guess that'd be me. You can learn a lot just by watching people. Over the years I've acquired quite a bit of material on why someone would want vengeance on this family."

Her eyes widened with interest. "*Vengeance* seems

like a strong word."

"So is *murder*."

Keisha held up her hand. "Wait—are you saying a member of the Eyler family murdered someone?"

Only now did I notice the tapping of my foot, the quiver of my leg. I gripped my knobby knee, willing it to stop. "You could say that. Though I don't have solid proof."

"And the plot thickens…"

"Oh yes, thick as my father's hair. Full head of it until the day he died." I chuckled, gesturing at my own nearly bald head. I was the unfortunate progeny who inherited my uncle's receding hairline.

"So you've got a pretty good idea of who killed the Eylers?"

"Not just an idea. I'm certain."

"How can you be so sure? According to the police report, there were no motives, no evidence, no witnesses."

I waved her assumptions away. "Oh, but there was one witness. A witness who never got the chance to speak out. Except to me."

Help me, the ghost implored again in the back of my mind.

In this moment I knew how to silence it. Keisha was the key, and I was the lock. Once I told her my story, she could finally exhume and free the ghosts who tormented me. They sought justice, so justice I would give them.

A HOUSE OF RUIN

Part 1

Keisha Fenty: "When the Eyler Family Massacre happened back in November of 1982, you had been working at the estate for nearly a decade by then. So it must have come as quite a shock that anyone would want to kill this family, considering all they had done for the community. Not only did Mr. Eyler represent some of the biggest authors in science-fiction and fantasy, but his wife founded several literacy nonprofits. But being the estate manager, you would know more than anyone what happened behind closed doors. Can you share a little about what the family was *really* like when no one was watching?"

Derl Newman: "Oh, if only walls could talk. There's a lot about this family that no one knows, and I only caught glimpses of the shadows that surrounded them. They had a darkness in them, all of them. Even the kids. But it all starts with the father, Tony Eyler. Long before my time there. But I heard the rumors. And in 1979, I discovered what he had done—what *they* had done. The whole brood. The kind of people they were beneath the philanthropic façade. You see, when you make a deal with the devil, you're bound to get burned by the flames."

Chapter 2

June 1979

I didn't make it a habit to root through my boss's dark secrets, but today I made an exception. I had no choice, after what I'd overheard. The low conspiratorial tones between Mr. Eyler—I wasn't permitted to call him *Tony*, not to his face, at least—and some unknown voice on the other end of the avocado green rotary phone couldn't be true. But then again, I knew more about Tony's true nature than most of his so-called friends or colleagues. And that terrified me.

"His blood is on your hands too, you know," Mr. Eyler said into the receiver, pressed close to his lips. It could have been an innocent turn of phrase if not for what followed.

"My career—my whole life—relies on your silence." From inside his den Mr. Eyler's voice grew low, urgent. "As does yours. You're an accomplice, and no number of years can erase your part in what happened. We both know I'm not the only one who benefited from his death."

Shortly after he hung up, Mr. Eyler rushed out of his office past me, his fashionable cognac leather briefcase bumping against his leg. He paused before descending the stairs to turn and address me.

"Derl, I've got to make a run into the city."

"On a Saturday, sir?"

"Duty calls. Let my wife know I'll be home late tonight, and tell the chef he's on call for a late dinner."

I nodded understanding.

There was no *thanks* or *please* when it came to Tony Eyler, not with his staff, nor his wife, nor his colleagues. Tony Eyler didn't ask, he commanded. I watched the back of his rust-colored paisley silk shirt and cream polyester pants descend the stairs, wondering how he managed to beat the heat in clothing far too warm for this summer day.

I glanced at my OMEGA Constellation watch, an original 1952 design, the leather worn soft by long service upon my father's wrist. It was the most expensive thing I owned, gifted to me from my father on his deathbed. Although the Pittsburgh steel mills had afforded Dad and our family a relatively comfortable life, lung cancer had stolen his last breath. According to the time, I still had a couple hours before Mrs. Eyler returned with the children.

She had taken them to see *The Muppet Movie* at The Oaks Theater, an escape offering central air conditioning on this hot, humid day, followed by a trip to McDonald's for a Happy Meal. The kids had been begging to try this latest addition to the fast-food menu, after all their school friends had bragged about the McDoodler stencil toy inside. I couldn't imagine the appeal of the wagon-train-themed meal in a box, but kids had always been something of a mystery to me.

After arranging the dinner schedule with the chef, I tiptoed across Mr. Eyler's office, cracking open the desk drawer he didn't know I had a key to. Between the shuffle of folders and my held breath, I glanced out the office window down onto the sprawling gardens lush with summer color that surrounded the orange brick driveway. While I rooted through each drawer, I listened for the echoing footsteps of the family returning home, or the children's chatter over who had the best Happy Meal toy. The grandfather clock in the corner ticked off each passing minute, but no one came. Not a single sound cut the eerie silence, save the rustle of my fingers rifling through documents.

After another handful of minutes I began to give up. If there was anything incriminating, he certainly wouldn't leave it here for anyone to find. I put everything away where I'd found it, for Tony was nothing if not attentive to detail. Rounding the desk, I paused at the doorway and turned to face the den, hoping something, anything, would stand out. That's when I found the smoking gun I was searching for, not in some secret hiding place, but right out in the open. The last place one would ever expect.

A sliver of dying sunlight sparkled against the glass hanging smack dab on the wall, for all the world to see. As if he *wanted* to get caught. How many times had I passed by this framed newspaper article, never realizing until now what it signified: my boss was a killer.

My breath fogged the glass as I leaned toward it. The article, dated June 1971, marked a major milestone in Mr. Eyler's publishing career. A two-column photo captured a younger version of my boss smiling broadly and shaking the hand of the then CEO of New York's top literary agency as he accepted his new promotion.

I pulled the frame down from the wall and read the article in its entirety:

> A new name has stolen the publishing world spotlight after the shocking loss of the agency's top literary agent in a bus-related accident that took his life last week. With a background in accounting and contracts, Tony Eyler has taken the position of Senior Agent in an unprecedented six-figure deal, where he'll be representing some of the top names in the literary world.

Accident, my ass.

Part of the article, the part that interested me most, had been folded over underneath it. I flipped the frame over, searching the back. Fiddling with several tiny clips that held it in place, it finally came free, scattering a thin stack of papers across the floor. Picking up a loose page, I immediately understood one thing: I held in my hands the answer to whose blood stained Mr. Eyler's hands, and what exactly he stood to gain from it.

Tucked between articles about President Richard Nixon's newly inaugurated "War on Drugs" and French daredevil Philippe Petit's groundbreaking (no pun intended) high wire walk between the towers of Notre-Dame Cathedral, one specific headline from the June 27, 1971, clipping gripped me:

TOP NEW YORK LITERARY AGENT DIES IN DEADLY BUS ACCIDENT

An image of the smiling victim, Scott Orson, accompanied the suspicious circumstances of his death.

While standing at a busy New York City intersection, the article detailed, the Mr. Orson tripped and fell in front of an oncoming bus and was instantly crushed to death. His personal assistant, none other than Tony Eyler, was quoted as saying, "It all happened so fast. One moment he was standing beside me, the next he just stepped out. I tried to stop him, but I wasn't fast enough."

That single moment catapulted *Personal Assistant*

Tony Eyler upward into a skyscraping corner office as *Senior Literary Agent* Tony Eyler when he took over his dead boss's client list. Being the smooth talker I knew Mr. Eyler to be, I imagined it wasn't too tough to steal the position from some other up-and-coming and perhaps more deserving applicant. After all, Mr. Eyler knew the ins and outs of his boss's job. He knew Scott's clients personally. He helped handle their projects. With the right half-truths and manipulation, which were second nature to my Machiavellian boss, his ascension would have been a piece of cake.

Kneeling on the floor, I skimmed the scattered articles, which further documented Scott's death and the subsequent investigation. It had started innocently enough as the funeral arrangements were publicly announced:

Funeral Draws Biggest Names in Modern Literature

But soon the police inquiry turned up details that had been buried, along with motives for possible suicide:

Investigation into Star Literary Agent's Death Uncovers Embezzlement Scheme

One clipped article after another, I flipped through the pile, unfolding a series of mysteries behind Scott's death that even to me seemed obvious red flags. Embezzled money that investigators discovered in a secret but not well-hidden account under his very own name. The inherited posthumous wealth that his wife denied knowing about. Conflicting witness accounts of the accident. Tragic accident, or a last resort death wish?

The media latched on to the story, still emptyhanded of answers:

NYPD QUESTIONS MOTIVE BEHIND AGENT'S 'ACCIDENT'

POLICE SUSPECT SUICIDE IN RENOWNED AGENT'S DEATH

With millions in stolen funds easily found and recovered, the media speculated that perhaps the agent was overcome by guilt for his embezzling crimes. Tony Eyler had planned the perfect setup to explain why Scott would have killed himself. But I knew, and his wife knew, that Scott was innocent:

WIFE OF PROMINENT AGENT SEEKS TRUTH ABOUT
HUSBAND'S DEATH

Only one person had the accounting expertise to embezzle money, the ruthless nature to take what he wanted, and the manipulative genius to pull it off: Tony Eyler.

In the eyes of one who knew Tony Eyler, saw his darkness seeping into everything he touched, every disturbing revelation led back to my boss. A man with no soul and the world to gain. All it took was some financial maneuvering and one little push into an oncoming bus.

A scrape of footsteps on the stairs startled me. The time on the grandfather clock showed that hours had passed. I leapt to my feet, peeked around the doorframe as the steps grew louder. I didn't need to see Tony to know it was him; I'd recognize the sound of his confident tread anywhere.

A wisp of a summer breeze swept up the staircase, catching the sepia newspaper clipping in my hand. It fluttered to the floor, joining the pile of incriminating evidence at my feet. I closed the door softly. If Tony caught me searching into his past, there was no telling what he would do to me. Especially now that I knew what he had already done once before.

Dropping back to my knees, I scrambled to sweep the papers back into the frame, with a single thought driving me: I was a dead man. I had no idea what order the newspaper clippings had been in, and there was no time to organize them now. Based on the echo, the footsteps were just down the hallway.

I considered throwing the frame to the floor and pretending the mess resulted from my bumping it in passing, and knocking it off the wall. But Tony would question what I was doing in his office in the first place while he was out, and the Master of Lies certainly knew how to detect them.

My fingers worked in overdrive. Shoving the pile into the frame, I straightened them as best I could and slid the back onto the frame. I pressed the first tab, but it wouldn't secure. The papers were too thick, pushing the back open. I readjusted it again, noting that the footsteps had paused somewhere near one of the bedrooms a couple doors down. He was just moments away.

"Derl?" Tony's voice boomed right outside the den. My heart thumped so hard I was certain it would seize up.

I rearranged the pages, flattening them even more, then replaced the backing. The footsteps resumed. I was going to get caught. Just as Tony's shadow passed under the doorsill, I jammed down the first tab, then the remaining ones as fast as my fingers could go. By the time I hung the frame back up, Tony was opening the door, eyes trained on me with a distrustful glare.

"Everything okay, boss?" I asked, straightening the picture frame as if I hadn't just been uncovering my boss's homicidal past.

"What are you doing in here?" he asked.

"Oh, I was just emptying the trash can. It's garbage day tomorrow."

"You're the estate manager, Derl; I don't pay you good money to empty the trash. Isn't that the maid's job? I forget her name."

It was rare that he could remember the names of *anyone* on his staff. I suppose I should have been flattered that he always seemed to remember mine, but then, as the estate manager, I was in charge of the staff, and the repository of his wrath when any little thing went awry.

"Annette. Yes, I'm afraid she must have overlooked your office. I'll speak to her about it, sir."

"See that you do."

I hated the idea of almost getting Annette in Dutch, but I needed to cover my ass, as the saying goes, and Tony would soon forget the incident. Luckily, he was too busy being a pompous jerk to realize that garbage day was actually yesterday.

"Reading something interesting?" he asked.

My brain froze. Had he caught me? A jumble of thoughts attempted to organize into something coherent, without success.

Tony gestured to the frame and sidled next to me. "I noticed you looking at this. That was the biggest day of my life."

I snatched a breath of relief. "Oh, right. Yes, I was admiring this article about you."

It was now as I gazed up at it that I noticed the page was crooked, revealing a hint of another article beneath it. As Tony stood beside me, examining the clipping, I couldn't blink. Couldn't move. I just waited for him to make the same discovery.

But he didn't. Instead he grinned, looked over at me, and said, "That day was the catalyst for everything I now have. You can't just wait around for luck to happen.

Sometimes you've got to make your own luck happen."

What I heard, however, as I grabbed the garbage can on my way out was:

Watch your ass, Derl, or maybe I'll push you in front of a bus too.

Chapter 3

October 1979

My finger trembled, hovering over the rotary dial above the 1. I had already swung the dial to the 9 and 1, then hesitated. Nothing about this felt right.

"Are you certain, ma'am, that we should be involving the police? This feels more like a situation for animal control," I suggested.

Across the parlor, sitting on the sofa clutching her youngest daughter Jennifer to her bow blouse, Jill glared at me. "The neighbor's dog attacked Jennifer." It was always *Jennifer,* never *Jenny* or *Jen,* for Jill Eyler didn't believe in nicknames or abbreviations; propriety was of utmost importance at the Eyler Estate. "Of course I'm going to involve the police and have that beast shot. And the owner should be in jail for not properly training that canine menace!"

Attacked. Beast. Menace. Jill's word choices showed off her flair for the dramatic.

Pressing a warm wet rag to Jennifer's thumbprint-sized scrape that grazed her elbow, Jill tended to the girl like she was bleeding out. Not a bloody drip stained Jill's burnt orange top that complimented her red hair, nor a stray teardrop soaked her jade sateen slacks. I couldn't imagine wanting to give a death sentence to an animal over a nip. To Jill, her children could do no wrong. But I saw. I observed. I knew just how spoiled rotten the children could be. And just how greedy for attention they were, even if it meant a dog was put down or an innocent man was jailed.

"I think you need to speak with the neighbor first," I suggested. "He said that Sprocket only jumped up to lick her face and Jennifer fell. The dog didn't bite her."

Jill gestured toward the flesh-white scrape. It was barely pink now. "And you believe him? He's clearly lying, Derl. Regardless, my daughter is going to be traumatized for life, and I'd rather it be taken care of now before something even worse happens next time."

I couldn't imagine what she thought was worse than a dog's friendly kiss.

"I'm just saying it's probably not wise to make enemies with your neighbor when he meant no harm. How about you let me handle it instead, and I'll make sure the dog stays off your property going forward?"

Jill's jaw tightened as she considered my offer, then softened before she spoke. "Alright, I'll let you deal with it this time. But if I ever see that dog on my property again, there's a 9mm upstairs and a bullet with Sprocket's name on it."

While we had dodged a bullet—literally—this time, I knew Jill Eyler meant every word she threw at me. Convincing the neighbor, a Vietnam War vet with a temper to match Jill's Irish one, to back down from this fight was another matter altogether.

"Thank you, ma'am." I headed to the wide entryway, out the polished oak double front doors where the front porch wrapped from one corner of the house to the other.

Crisp air filled my lungs. Autumn at the Eyler Estate was breathtaking. Surrounded by six acres of woods, lit on fire by brilliant goldenrod and rosy sunlight, it brought me to awe every time I stepped on the gaping porch that stretched long enough to fit two suites of cushioned balsa wood patio furniture, with plenty of space to spare.

When the Eylers first acquired the mansion, they had been living a state away in New York City, the hub of the publishing world. I say *acquired* because that is exactly what the Eylers lived for: to acquire things. Wealth. Power. Respect. Mansions.

Even people, such as myself.

Don't misunderstand me. I was paid well in my capacity as estate manager, and enjoyed a sumptuous suite of rooms in the mansion along with the freedom to wear what I wanted, like the Ralph Lauren red and charcoal tracksuit I was currently sporting. If it were not for that fact, I would have told Mr. Eyler exactly where he could shove that wealth, power, and respect.

I often wondered if this home purchase was a shoutout to the world about their new status among the elite, a reputation most prized by Jill Eyler.

Built in 1880 by a wealthy glass manufacturing couple, the home had quite a storied history. The descendants of the original family—coincidentally, a father, mother, and three kids, like the Eylers—died in a suspicious house fire in 1956. Luckily the flames destroyed few parts of the dwelling, leaving most of the bones salvageable. For years it remained uninhabited and left to decay, and was home to a family of squatters for a time. Tragically, that family was also found dead in this house, frozen to death.

Jill Eyler had first laid eyes upon the house when she was a little girl. The family, natives of Pittsburgh, had taken a Sunday afternoon drive to the suburbs and found themselves in the quaint town. Venturing onto a country road, the "storybook palace," as Jill called it, had appeared as if by magic. She instantly fell in love with the three-story architectural masterpiece. In 1972, on a visit home to see her parents, she'd driven out to see the "storybook palace" again and was sad to see it had fallen into disrepair, though it retained much of the ornate woodwork, countless original fixtures, and multiple fireplaces. On a whim she purchased it on foreclosure, pouring quite a bit of money into renovating it to fit its original era, from the cherub paintings on the atrium ceiling, to the crown molding in the parlor. Ironically, her favorite room, untouched by the flames, was the library, the same room in which she would take her final breath.

Initially the home was intended as a second residence closer to Jill's family in Pittsburgh. Yet each trip back to New York, it grew harder and harder to leave the estate, until one day she simply stayed. It became her full-time residence with the children and a full-time staff, while Mr. Eyler remained in New York during the week and spent his weekends in the Steel City.

Eventually the mansion wasn't enough to satiate Jill's appetite for *more*.

Along with the impressive home, Jill Eyler demanded an impressive name. A royal name. Shortly after I came on to help manage the estate, *Mrs.* Jill Eyler became *Duchess* Jill Eyler. At least she didn't require me to call her Your Royal Highness.

Who knew one could purchase a royal title from the tiny Principality of Sealand? The notion of the former British fortress island being a *principality* was generous (it was actually a concrete and steel construction located seven miles off the UK coast), as was Sealand's offer to let any Tom, Dick, or Harry purchase a royal title. But when Jill discovered she could obtain a noble title, and all the grandiose documentation to prove it, she jumped at the chance. Vanity and a deep desire for respect ran deep in the Eyler blood. With enough money, one could buy virtually anything.

Except for the goodwill of Sprocket's owner, Sam,

who was currently storming up the driveway toward me, his striped polyester shirt showing a sliver of bare chest.

"We gotta confab, Derl!" Sam grumbled as he approached.

"My man, Sam. I'm really sorry about Mrs. Eyler's overreaction—"

The index finger Sam jabbed against my chest cut my apology short. "Don't try to cover for them, Derl. You and I both know that family is trippin'. I always see the lady giving me the hairy eyeball when I pass, as if they're better than me."

"I understand, but—"

"And her kid's jive-talking, accusing Sprocket of biting her. She was throwing rocks at her, that mean little devil spawn! Sprocket wasn't even on her property, by the way. She was in *my* yard, so technically that kid was trespassing! So if that lady's going to come at me threatening animal control, she's got another thing coming."

I raised my hands in surrender. "Hey, I get it, man. I'm not condoning anything the Eylers did. I'm just trying to smooth things over. You know I can't afford to get fired over this, the way the economy is right now."

"Let me give you the skinny, Derl. I don't want you to lose your job, but if they don't take a chill pill, it *will* get ugly."

We were getting nowhere with this conversation. "Tell, me, Sam, what can I do to help fix this?"

Sam shook his head, his long hair brushing his shoulders, and he propped his hands on his hips, where a belt holster hugged the barrel of a pistol. For several minutes he paced the gravel parking area, mumbling, "First they draft my ass and send me to Nam where I nearly get my friggin' head blown off, then I come home to shit like this." Finally the crunch of his platform shoes stopped, he turned to me, and aimed that trigger finger right back at me again. "If they keep their distance, I'll keep mine. But if they ever come after me or my dog again, I swear to you, Derl, it's war."

Considering Sam had survived the battle of Hamburger Hill and lived to tell the tale, this could get dicey.

"I'll do everything in my power to keep the good vibes, Sam," I assured him.

"I gotta skitty." Assuaged for now, Sam stormed off, his bell bottoms rustling a trail of fallen leaves before I could get another word in, not that any more words I had would have helped.

I realized then that while the Eylers were hiding in their fortress, building their legacy of wealth and power, outside of it, the enemies they'd made were plotting to bring their empire down.

Part 2

Keisha Fenty: "When the murder first made the news, the police had withheld most of the details due to the gruesome nature of the crime. Now it's time the truth came out. Tell the world what it's dying to know: what did you see when you walked into the library that day?"

Derl Newman: "Like every good horror story, it happened on a dark and stormy night."

Keisha Fenty: "You're kidding, right?"

Derl Newman: "Yes, just trying to lighten the mood. This isn't easy for me, you know."

Keisha Fenty: "I know. Take your time, Derl."

Derl Newman: "It was early evening dark, just after dinner when the sun began to set, as it does in November. A snowstorm had blanketed the Eyler Estate…"

Chapter 4

IF WALLS COULD TALK

November 29, 1982

The sky had been apocalyptic red that morning, reflecting pink off the untouched snow. My father would have recited the old adage, "Red sky at night, sailors' delight. Red sky in the morning, sailors take warning." Seemed like Dad had a corny quote for every occasion. How I wished I could hear again his clear tenor voice ringing out with the bawdy songs he and his iron workers union buddies sang over a beer when their shift was done. And yet today I would hear only the empty silence of loss.

Over the weekend I had taken my mother's ashes downstate to the rural outskirts of Pennsylvania Amish country, to the cabin where I had spent countless summers at as a child. Yesterday, in the same farewell gesture I had years ago given my dad, I opened the urn so Mom could catch Dad on a bitter breeze as she floated away. "No funeral for me," she had once told me after my father died. "Use whatever you would spend on a memorial to take yourself somewhere warm and exotic in my memory." I had never had the money to take Mom somewhere warm and exotic in her life; I was certainly not going to enjoy it in her death.

The bloody sky should have been warning enough to stay away, but I didn't heed it. Instead, I shook the snow off my boots as I stepped up to the Eylers' front door, aiming the key toward the lock. But when I grabbed the doorknob, it turned easily, swinging the unlocked doors open. A little unusual for this early hour, for this late-sleeping family, but still no warning bells clanged.

The house was devoid of activity or noise. It was quite possible they had gone to visit Mrs. Eyler's parents who lived in the city, so I shrugged it off. While I had run into the gardener on my way in, none of the other house staff were scheduled to work, due to a long holiday weekend after the exhausting preparation for the Eyler's annual Thanksgiving gala. All of the fireplace hearths were cold and empty, so I started a fire in the living room before tending to my duties in my office tucked on the other side of the house where the former servants' quarters had been.

Hours passed without the appearance of a single soul. Eventually, curiosity drew me upstairs to the children's bedrooms. I peeked first into Charlotte's open bedroom door, noting the perfectly made bed. Again, a little unusual for this sloppy teenager. I headed to Dustin's room one door down, his door also ajar. Another empty bed. And lastly was Jennifer's bedroom, a crayoned

"Princesses Only" sign taped to the front of her closed door. The doorknob clicked as I twisted it open and pushed, finding her purple room dark and empty.

Turning toward the banister that ran along the hallway, I searched the house for any sign of life. Only the crackle of fire chewing away the wood downstairs disturbed the hush.

Walking across the first floor, and up the stairs, I heard the grandfather clock chime six times. It was suppertime, when I always fed Styx, the cat. But he did not come bolting toward the kitchen as he always did in Pavlovian response to the chimes.

Something was wrong.

"Styx!" I yelled to the empty house. The crazed feline, black like the River Styx, loathed everyone but me, and always responded with a broken meow when I called him. Countless cans of 9Lives Chicken and Tuna Dinner had bought me his affection early on when I first found him wandering the surrounding woods. I listened for his scratchy yowl, wondering where he might have gotten himself stuck. On many occasions I had found him locked in a closet or underneath a kitchen cabinet, but his muted cry always let me know where he was.

Silence was definitely unusual for this cat, for this Monday evening. Now this was spooky.

I could imagine the family heading to Jill's parents' home for the weekend, but taking the cat with them? Absolutely not. If Styx hadn't inserted himself as a permanent fixture in the house, and allowed him to remain more or less as my pet—with all of the attendant responsibilities—Jill would have already gotten rid of him. After the first and last time he scratched Jennifer for picking him up by the tail, Styx became kitty non grata to the Eylers. And he knew better than to be caught by anyone, lest he get tossed outside. Styx was fortunate enough to have 9,000 square feet to hide in.

A thump on the ceiling arrested my attention from the missing cat. I headed up the third flight of stairs, everything growing darker as I entered the belly of the house, untouched by natural light. The library door stood closed at the end of the dark hallway. When I reached the door, my palm cupping the doorknob, another startling thump came from within.

I swung open the door and turned on the light, totally unprepared for the gruesome scene that greeted me. I'm embarrassed to admit that the scream that poured out of me belonged more to a terrified child than a grown man.

Five bodies lying on the floor. I recognized them as Tony, Jill, Charlotte, Dustin, and Jennifer, posed in the shape of a crude pentagram. Upon each face lay an open book. The children's pajamas, the parents' clothes stained with dried blood. Bodies stiff with rigor mortis. My knees weakened then gave in as I gripped the doorjamb to stay upright.

Despite my revulsion, my curiosity got the better of me and I crept toward Tony's body. Upon his face rested

The Hobbit, so I lifted the spine of the book and peeked under it, wondering what it was hiding.

"What the hell!" I yelped, dropping the book and stumbling backward so fast I fell on my ass.

The murderer had taken a trophy—Tony's right eye, leaving a gaping hole in his head. The image of the remaining blue orb gazing sightlessly back at me would haunt my nights forevermore.

With my back pressed against the bookshelf, I closed my eyes, searched for air, steadied my racing mind. Finally my gasps calmed to shaky breaths. I clawed my way back to my feet. I scrambled toward the library telephone to summon the police, when a wail shattered my very last nerve. Dropping the receiver to the floor, I spun around to find Styx, circling his lithe body around a bust of Edgar Allan Poe, his tail puffed and pupils engulfing the yellow.

Relief passed over me that Styx was alive and well, until my gaze settled back on the family near the hearth, noting something I hadn't seen before. Open sores on various body parts—a finger here, a neck there. Upon closer inspection, I realized they weren't sores at all. Starving over the weekend, Styx had...started eating them.

My stomach churned; I was swimming in nausea. I wanted to look away, erase the visual of gnawed-away flesh from my memory. But I couldn't tear my gaze from it. It was as if it was my burden as caretaker of this family that I should endure every awful moment of this with them.

With my stare still fixed on the family, I reached behind me, hands groping blindly for the coiled telephone cord dangling near my thigh. I couldn't stand to be in this room another minute. Whatever had happened in this room, it was clearly an act of rage, and as I dialed the police, I suddenly wondered if the killer was still here. In this house. And if I would be next.

A HOUSE OF RUIN

Part 3

Derl Newman: "As it would turn out, I wasn't next. Although as you know, the taking of trophies and the ritualistic placement of the books seemed to indicate the calling cards of a serial killer. But no one ever killed in that bizarre manner again. Even today I have a terrifying feeling that the killer will come back to send one final message, and I'll be the conduit for that message."

Keisha Fenty: "What do you think the killer's message was?"

Derl Newman: "That would depend on who did it. Each of the house staff had a legitimate grudge against the family. But murder is a vicious cycle. You can't figure out *who* until you figure out *why*, and you need the *why* to figure out the *who*."

Keisha Fenty: "It's been forty years and investigators were never able to crack this case. Yet you claim to know the *who* and *why*."

Derl Newman: "I do indeed. Because I saw everything

that happened in this house on a day-to-day basis, and I knew each staff member intimately—their secrets, their vices, their pasts. You want to know who committed this grisly act? Well, let me first introduce you to the suspects, and let's see if you can figure it out for yourself."

Chapter 5

January 1982

The older you get, the thinner your tolerance becomes. Or in my case, my hair. Though, looking back on that blizzard-besieged January afternoon, I'm not certain that Martin Poe, butler to the Eyler family, ever had any tolerance to begin with.

One couldn't necessarily fault him for this At nearly fifty years old, embarking on a new career as a chauffeur, staff organizer, to-do list keeper, and sometimes babysitter was asking a bit much from the divorced, childless former tattoo artist. But the early 1980s recession hit his business too hard to recover, sending him to the unemployment line along with millions of others. Since the Eylers were desperate enough to hire him after a slew of previous butlers had quit (the Eyler children made Dennis the Menace look tame), Martin figured a firm hand was all he needed to set these kids straight.

The Eyler children quickly changed his mind.

Unlike Benson, the dapper, acid-tongued Black butler in the popular sitcom of the same name, Martin looked more like an Ozzy Osbourne roadie than a domestic worker. And he absolutely loathed children. As the only son of a widowed mother, whom he idolized and adored, and who was the likely reason for his divorce, perhaps he simply wasn't exposed to children enough. But then again, the Eyler kids were a different breed.

I'd noticed Martin's unease the day he first set foot on the Eyler Estate, unpacking his bags and warning the children to stay out of his room. Out of his stuff. And especially out of his closet where his most personal possessions were kept: an autographed Journey poster, his father's Swiss Army knife that held great sentimental value, and a photo album celebrating his life with his mother.

It was a small request as far as he was concerned, but an impossible one for eight-year-old Jennifer Eyler.

As long as the children stayed out of his way, he all but ignored them. Avoided them when he could. But he was the butler, and a butler's job at the Eyler Estate was to tend to the demands of the three little hellions that lived here. He did his job, but it was usually accompanied by a grumble under his breath, or a whispered swear word that of course Jennifer would overhear and tattle to her mother about. He tolerated it as best he could. Until it all came to a head this January afternoon.

School had been cancelled due to inclement weather.

With several feet of snow burying cars and holding families hostage in their homes, even the snowplows couldn't keep up with the snowfall. Mix that with the steep Pennsylvania hills and black ice, and the journey was simply too perilous to risk lives kids' lives. Little did Mr. and Mrs. Eyler know their children's lives were at a greater risk being stuck home with Martin Poe.

Unlike the other staff (myself being the exception) who didn't have room and board at the estate, Martin had agreed to take one of the eight bedrooms during the week, returning to his apartment only on weekends. There he shared 500 square feet with a roommate who left nail clippings on the floor, cigarette butts on the coffee table, and dirty dishes beside the sink—never *inside* the sink, Martin often lamented. Thus, the arrangement allowed Martin to come and go enough that he never quite got irritated enough with either living situation to go batshit crazy.

Until today.

Perhaps it was the damp cold that saturated the bones of the old mansion. Or Charlotte's moody tirade (as she glared accusingly at Jennifer) over *someone* stealing her brand-new Walkman and David Bowie cassette tape that she'd gotten for Christmas. Or Dustin's whining that his new *Asteroids* video game for his Atari was *"borrrrring"* (and demanded a new game). Or Jennifer's latest prank filling Martin's shampoo bottle with Slime (then complaining that she ran out of Slime).

Whatever it was, the moment Martin's stud-bedecked black boots stomped into his bedroom to find his mother's photo album split open on the floor, pictures thrown in piles beside Jennifer's crossed legs as she drew permanent marker devil horns and facial hair on his beloved deceased mother's face, ice flooded his blue eyes. Rage surged through the veins popping up beneath the chain he wore on his neck. And the tiny blood vessel that creased his forehead between locks of wavy rock 'n' roll hair thrummed wildly.

"What the hell are you doing?" he yelled. Martin fell to his knees on the floor, searching through the jumble for a single unharmed picture. Photo after photo was ruined. His memory of his mother was tainted by scribbled horns and Hitler mustaches.

He shot up from the floor, throwing the pictures down and stooping to yell in her face. "How could you?" His fingers, tattooed with the letters AC/DC, closed in on her sweatered arm.

"You can't tell me what to do! My mom's your boss." Jennifer's pink tongue popped out between her lips as she blew a raspberry at him.

"You little shit..." he muttered, ripping her away from the stack of photographs she was still defacing.

"Ouch! You're hurting me!" she screeched. Instant tears poured down her chubby cheeks.

But that only made Martin tighten his grip on her, as he yanked her out of his bedroom and dragged her like a ragdoll into the hallway where I had been watching, dumbstruck with horror.

"You think you can just ruin my stuff and get away with it? It's time someone teaches you a lesson, kid." Over the years I had heard annoyance in his tone, but never this kind of maniacal, red-faced fury. As I looked on in disbelief, he dragged the little girl kicking and screaming over to the banister. I could only guess at his intent.

"Martin, no!"

I grabbed the cuff of his leather jacket just as he was about to lift the child. Meanwhile Jill Eyler rushed up the stairwell, gawking at the scene. Martin's eyes met mine. As if my stare drained his anger, he freed the girl to stumble into her mother's embrace.

I glanced down where I held him firmly, his sleeve slipping up his forearm, and I released him. But not before I caught a glimpse of something stamped onto his skin—the same image the killer would leave ten months later.

"Mommy, he hurt me!" Jennifer wailed into Jill's shoulder.

"How dare you touch my daughter!" Jill screamed above Jennifer's head that she protectively pressed to her chest.

"She was destroying pictures of my mother—pictures I can't replace," Martin protested. "Derl, you saw what she did." Martin shot me a beseeching look.

I raised my hands in surrender and stepped back, not wanting to get involved. If there was anything I learned throughout my tenure at the Eyler Estate, it was never to get involved.

"I don't care what she did. You had no right to touch her." The hand that stroked Jennifer's hair trembled. Her eyes snapped with fury. "She's just a baby! You're lucky I don't call the police...and I still might!"

Martin shook his head. There was no reasoning with her. "What kind of monster have you raised that enjoys being so cruel?"

Jill's jaw dropped. "*You* are calling my child a monster? Don't make me laugh. You're the monster. I mean, look at you, you Satan-worshipping freak! I don't know why my husband ever hired a low-life like you! I was against it all along. Get out of my house...now!"

I had come to discover by this point that Jill was a one-strike-and-you're-out kind of boss. There were no second chances when it came to the Eylers.

"You're firing me for this?" Martin stepped up to Jill, the top of her teased red hair barely brushing his pecs.

"I'll do a lot more than fire you if you don't leave this instant."

"With all due respect, Mrs. Eyler," I cut in, "Martin has been an exemplary employee. He is punctual and conscientious, and this is the only time I recall his ever having lost his temper— despite the numerous provocations to do so in such a, shall we say, dynamic household. If you ask me—"

"No one did ask you, Derl!" Jill spat. "Mind your place, or I'll fire you too." She turned to Martin. "Now, get out!"

"Fine. I'll grab my stuff and go. I don't have to take this shit from you people."

Jill pressed her hand against his chest. "No, I'll have it packed up and mailed to you. Leave. This instant."

While still shaken by a side of Martin I'd never seen, I also felt bad for him in that moment. His only photos of his beloved mother completely ruined, his job and home lost because he'd understandably lost his cool. And his pride crushed beneath the tiny foot of an eight-year-old girl who smirked triumphantly up at him from her mother's bosom.

"You'll regret this," he warned as he turned to leave.

"Not as much as you'll regret hurting my daughter," Jill spat back. "See if you ever find work in this state again. I'll make sure you suffer for this."

Martin paused at the landing and turned to face her. "Oh, we'll see about that. Watch your back, because I won't forget this. And neither will you."

As he blustered down the stairs, the leather cuff hugged his forearm, still revealing the image that would sear my brain. The same shape I would walk in to find the Eyler family arranged in: a pentagram.

Ten months later I would wonder if he had made good on his threat.

Chapter 6

February 1982

Carrie Spacek was a wee slip of a thing. Wiry but tough, like a steel rod. Despite her tiny hands and cadaverous arms, she could pull weeds twice the size of her body, and she was ruthless with her shears.

As tough as she was in the garden, she had a gentle heart that easily bled. That was often the curse of those who indulged in the arts. Her garden beds were her art. Her flower arrangements were her art. The stories she regaled the Eyler children with were her art. But this very trait—her tender heart and creative soul—as I would discover this starry February evening, would become her biggest threat. And eventually the Eylers' biggest threat as well.

Silver moonlight lit a path from the outdoor shed to the dormant rose garden near the front of the house. I had been helping Carrie haul mulch to the various flowerbeds.

"Gotta protect those roots through tonight's harsh

temperature," Carrie had explained, insisting the job couldn't wait until daylight.

I didn't care about roots, but I cared about Carrie getting her five-year-old daughter Shelly home at a decent hour. It wasn't every day that she was allowed to bring Shelly to work with her, but with school out on holiday, Mrs. Eyler had agreed—as long as Shelly didn't bother the Eyler kids. As far as I could tell, it was always the other way around.

"Thank you for helping me, Derl. You're a good friend." Carrie flashed me her demure grin. It was as if a more confident smile would pain her. "This should about do it."

"Happy to help, ma'am," I said, brushing the grit off my palms. The bitter temperature swept a chill over me, so I pulled my mohair scarf a little tighter until the soft fabric hugged my chin.

Plucking the pruning shears and shovel off the ground, I headed back to the shed where Shelly stood in a pocket of frost-kissed grass. The poor girl was dressed in little more than tatters, but I knew it was probably all Carrie could afford on her meager pay as a single mother. Light played on Shelly's strawberry blonde hair, a perfect miniature of her mother.

"Here, you need this more than I do." Unwrapping the scarf from around my neck, I circled it twice as many times around the child until her face was smothered in warmth. "Better?"

Shelly nodded eagerly, then hugged my legs. "Thank you, Mr. Derl." Her gratitude was muffled by mohair, which made me smile as she scampered off into the yard to watch the Eyler children play Flashlight Tag.

"What's wrong with her?" Dustin pointed to Shelly, arms out as she spun circles under the moonlight, chin thrust toward the sky.

I felt another presence approach behind me. "Oh, she's stargazing, honey," Carrie answered. It was a favorite pastime for Shelly.

"What's stargazing?" Jennifer asked, looking upward with a curious frown.

Carrie chuckled. "You've never heard of stargazing? It's when you search the night sky for stars and constellations."

"It looks stupid." Jennifer was clearly unimpressed.

Carrie's flaxen hair, pulled back in a low ponytail, looked like a silk stole cascading down her back. A turtleneck peeked up from her winter coat as she guided the Eyler children around the garden, pointing to the various constellations dotting the firmament.

"There's Cassiopeia," Carrie explained, pointing to a cluster of stars in the inky expanse above. "It looks like a big W."

I searched for this alleged W but couldn't find it, no matter how hard I looked.

Jennifer laughed. "Cassie *Pee*-a. Why'd they name it after pee?"

Carrie's lips rose in an ever-patient grin that only she among the house staff possessed. "Oh, no, dear, it's named after the myth of Queen *Cassiopeia*. You see, she was a vain queen, and that vanity was her downfall when she boasted that she was more beautiful than all the sea nymphs. Well, that was the wrong thing to say, because when the sea nymphs heard this, they wanted her punished by Poseidon, the sea god."

Carrie's voice grew conspiratorial as the story poured from her mouth in swirls of cloudy breath. "Poseidon agreed and sent a monster to destroy Queen Cassiopeia's kingdom. Seeing her kingdom coming to ruin, she begged a wise oracle for help, and the oracle told her that in order to appease Poseidon, she had to sacrifice her daughter Andromeda to the monster. Sadly she did so, leaving her daughter chained to a rock for the monster to find."

The children's eyes widened in shock.

"Mommy, did she die?" Shelly's voice wavered, her lower lip trembled as her little imagination ran wild, I supposed, with images of the daughter's destruction.

Carrie leaned down, hands on her knees, as she tapped Shelly's nose, rosy and drippy with cold. "Oh, it was close, but just as the monster was about to take the daughter, a god named Perseus passed by and rescued her!"

"Yay!" Shelly clapped her gloved hands.

"Perseus soon married the daughter, but at the wedding a fight broke out between her ex-boyfriend and

Perseus. The only way Perseus could defend himself was to chop off the head of Medusa, who had living snakes for hair, for once anyone looked directly at her, they instantly turned to stone. Unfortunately, Queen Cassiopeia also looked at Medusa and turned to stone. And that's when she was cast into the sky, where she was condemned to circle the celestial realm forever as punishment for her vanity and all the trouble she caused. That's what the W shows—her sitting upon her throne, always watching, looking down with a warning gaze so we never fall prey to vanity."

As a cloud passed across the moon, an eerie darkness enveloped us all in a moment of contemplation. It was a chilling story, for a chilly night, and yet I sensed a truth behind the myth. Always watching, always waiting. It was the nature of revenge.

Carrie's chipper voice yanked me from this ominous thought as she added, "If you follow the middle of the W, you can find the North Star." Carrie waved toward the sky.

"What's so great about the North Star?" Dustin's question was laced with mockery that Carrie didn't acknowledge.

"It's the anchor of the northern sky. For centuries it's helped travelers determine the right direction to go, because it glows so brightly. That's what makes it special—it's a beacon of inspiration and hope for the lost."

Dustin shrugged. "Sounds dumb to me."

"It's not dumb," Shelly squeaked in her mom's defense.

"You're dumb," Dustin retorted.

"Yeah, like anything you say matters, Shelly," Jennifer shot back. "You smell bad and have holes in your shoes. No one cares what you think, *Shmelly*."

"Kids, c'mon. That's enough." I ushered the children inside before things got out of hand. Carrie said something about wanting to get something from her car and trotted off with Shelly in tow.

By the time the Eyler kids had thrown off their winter wear in the entry and rumbled upstairs, Carrie had returned from her car carrying a thick stack of papers held together with a binder clip. I didn't ask what it was, but as she often did, Carrie took me into her confidence.

"It's my manuscript." Carrie nervously explained, holding it up with both hands. "I've been working on this for years. I thought maybe Mr. Eyler wouldn't mind reading it, since he's, y'know, a literary agent."

As she held the stack of papers out for me to read the cover page, I was distracted by a series of deep red lines, like festering claw marks, across her knuckles. A rash crept up her hand, coating her wrist and arm with inflamed pink hives. Carrie caught me staring.

"Oh, yeah," she said, "Styx got me when I tried to remove him from the garden shed a few days ago. I'm terribly allergic, and it takes forever to heal."

"Do you need something for it? Hydrocortisone cream?"

"That's okay. I'll treat it again when I get home. It eventually goes away." She scratched her neck, where an angry red irritation was spreading up toward her chin, which hadn't been noticeable in the moonlight. She covered it self-consciously with her infected hand. "That cat really hates me."

"Don't take it personally." I rested my hand on her shoulder. "Styx hates everyone but me."

"Do you think Mr. Eyler would be willing read my book?" Carrie asked.

The optimism rising in her question broke my heart, because I knew Tony Eyler a lot better than she did. He represented an exclusively male stable of authors and was of the moronic opinion that there were no good women writers. Carrie, as a "lowly" gardener and a female, had two strikes against her. I could never dash her positivity, though.

"I would hope so." And yet I knew such hope was too much to expect.

"My mommy's gonna sell a bunch of books!" Shelly proudly proclaimed from Carrie's hip.

Carrie chuckled, patting Shelly on top of her head. "Well, let's not get ahead of ourselves, sweetie. But that's what Mommy hopes will happen."

"Well, I think that's wonderful," I said. "Good luck with it." Knowing what little spare time Carrie had between her parenting and job demands, her dedication to her art spoke volumes.

Just then Mr. Eyler rounded the corner. His focus was fixed on the *Time* magazine he held, the headline "Unemployment: The Biggest Worry" splashed across the cover.

"Mr. Eyler, sorry to bother you," Carrie hesitantly said as she stepped toward him.

Tony barely paused, giving her a cursory glance.

"I was just wondering," Carrie continued, "if you could look at a novel I wrote. I completely understand if you don't have time, but I was hoping…maybe…y'know…" Carrie fumbled through her plea, but I could see that North Star hope sparkle in her eager hazel eyes.

Tony's face scrunched in confusion. "Wait, who are you?"

Carrie's confidence fell along with her smile. "Carrie Spacek, your gardener. I've been working for you for over five years now. And I wrote this book, a time-travel adventure where a young man goes back in time to save his family from a disaster that's about to happen. I think you might enjoy it—"

"You and every other shmuck," Tony cut in. "Time travel? Sounds like a flop idea to me, Callie."

"Carrie—"

"Look, writing isn't for you, honey. Give it up now before you get your precious little feelings hurt. I'm too

69

busy representing actual talent to waste my time on this." He paused his reprimand to give Shelly, then Carrie, a once-over. "From the looks of that rash, you should be more focused on taking care of whatever infection you're spreading." His wandering gaze finally settled on Shelly. "And how about provide your kid with decent clothes instead of chasing a pipe dream, Callie?"

A dreadful silence lingered as Tony Eyler left Carrie, pink with embarrassment, standing there in the entry, crestfallen. And poor Shelly knew the heartless man had shattered her mother's dreams. Carrie blinked her tears away as she grabbed Shelly's gloved hand in hers and led her to the front door, manuscript tucked under her arm.

"You may say I'm just chasing a pipe dream, *Mr.* Eyler," she muttered, "but someday you'll eat those words. Because one day I promise you, I'll be famous."

Nine months later, her prediction was fulfilled as her name was splashed upon the front page of every daily newspaper in the country, her face on every nightly newscast. Not for the book deal she craved, but as a murder suspect.

Chapter 7

THE MELODRAMATIC MAILMAN

May 1982

When you play with a fiery redhead, you're bound to get burned. And Jill Eyler burned everything she touched. Especially those who burned her first.

In this case it wouldn't be fire, but rather a gunshot. A gunshot ringing out from the backyard this gorgeous spring day jolted my attention from the accounting I had been handling that morning in my tiny stifling office in the former servant's quarters of the house adjacent to my suite of rooms. Picking up the receiver of the new ivory touch-tone phone Jill proudly purchased—*with speed dial!*—I had already punched the 9 on the keypad while listening for another shot.

After a minute or two of only the creak of the mansion's old bones shifting, I wheeled my chair around toward the open window. Sweet honeysuckle nectar saturated the air, and spring color—coral mandevilla, royal lilac, sapphire hydrangea—peppered the landscape. My gaze roved from the driveway over to the front porch, scanning for signs of life.

Parked near the side of the house, slightly out of view, was the mail truck. The same mail truck that was parked there every Tuesday and Thursday morning from 9:25 to 10:15. The postman's creed says: *Neither snow nor rain nor heat nor gloom of night stays these couriers from the swift completion of their appointed rounds*—it says nothing, however, about being detained by hot, forbidden sex. This was the little secret that Jill kept tucked away. But I knew. And the rest of the house staff knew it too.

Secrets didn't stay hidden long in a house full of eyes and ears.

I checked the time. Just shy of ten o'clock. It wasn't unusual that Wilson Farmiga was here, but a gunshot definitely was out of place on the grounds of the mansion. Despite his growing exotic firearm collection, Tony Eyler collected them mainly for bragging rights among his friends and colleagues, all of whom fancied themselves macho personalities of the Rambo variety.

When Wilson Farmiga hand delivered a package six months earlier, it became the first of many packages he'd give Jill Eyler—if you catch my drift. He was young. Adoring. Eager to please. Everything Jill's husband was not. So when this handsome, single mailman with the winsome smile showed up on her million-dollar doorstep, they both thought they had won the love lottery.

Wilson lavished her with all the attention and kisses

and caresses that she yearned for. And Jill lavished him with all the gifts and cash and favors that he yearned for. For months it went on like this, secret rendezvous before the kids got home from school, quickies between mail deliveries, and for a while they both considered it a win-win deal. As long as no one found out. Or asked for too much.

Well, as Jill was prone to want too much, the price of their affair soon demanded blood. And as bad luck would have it, their secret wasn't theirs to keep for long.

I had no idea who the gunshot had been intended for, or where—or in whom—the bullet might have landed. But gunshots mixed with an affair was a deadly combination.

Jumping up from my chair, I ran down the stairwell that led to the large patio overlooking the backyard. Near the far corner of the fenced yard, I watched as Jill wrestled with Wilson over the gun in her hand. She shoved him; he pulled her against him; she slapped him; and finally Wilson managed to snatch the weapon away.

"Give it back!" she yelled, pawing for it as Wilson, holding the gun behind his back, easily sidestepped her advances. Curiously, he held a piece of paper, flapping in the warm breeze, in his other hand.

"Calm down, babe!" Wilson pleaded.

Jill's face was as beet red as her hair. Her arms waved wildly while Wilson stood there dumbfounded. "I won't calm down until you give me the damn gun!" she screeched. She lunged for it again; Wilson backed away, gripping the gun tightly.

Catching the rich coffee color of the handle, and the black matte of the barrel, I recognized it as the Walther PPK 9mm Tony had recently acquired for his collection. The German-made, Nazi-issued relic was Tony's second pride and joy (number one, of course, being his first edition of *The Hobbit)*; it normally hung it in a glass case in the library, where all of his most prized possessions lived. It remained to be seen what Jill was doing with it.

"You could have shot me," Wilson said lamely.

"Good! And you would have deserved it, too. I was only trying to give it back to you when it went off. How the hell could I know it was loaded?"

"I had to show Mr. Eyler how to load it—with a Walther, it's a very tricky business. You should have checked the magaz—"

"Shut up! I can't believe you went and introduced yourself to Tony behind my back! He would kill us both if he found out about us. What were you thinking?" Jill propped her hands on her bony hips, demanding an answer.

"I'm thinking about our future, Jill. You know I love you and want to be with you," Wilson begged.

"There is no future for us, Wilson. And selling Tony this gun? You might as well have just stuck it in his hand so he could kill us both!"

"Well, he mentioned he's a collector when we were

talking, and that there gun was owned by a Gestapo officer. Plus the Walther PPK is James Bond's weapon of choice—which is pretty cool too. Tony paid me a fortune for it. Enough for us to get a place of our own. Isn't that what you want?"

Jill stomped a circle in the grass. "No! I wanted a little fun on the side, not a homicidal husband. I don't understand you at all. Do you have a death wish?"

"If I don't have you, then I guess I do. This letter"—Wilson held it up, shoving it in her face—"tells Tony everything. He needs to know about us."

Even from my vantage point across the yard, hidden under the shadow of the back porch roof, I could feel the fury in Jill's stare. She was daring Wilson to tell Tony, but he had no idea how much that dare would cost everyone.

Her threat was slow and steady. "If you tell Tony anything, you'll never see your mother again, Wilson. I know she's an illegal immigrant, and I can have INS at her front door faster than you can say *speed dial.*"

It was the only thing she needed to say. That simple warning would unravel Wilson's entire world. He lived *with* his mother, and he lived *for* his mother. (I'd overheard enough details during their sex afterglow conversations to fill a soap opera.)

"So that's it then? You just want to end what we have?" The heartbreak in Wilson's voice was palpable.

"You don't get it, do you? We don't *have* anything.

It's just sex, Wilson. Get over it. And give me back that stupid gun you sold Tony. If he sees it's missing, he'll be more pissed about that than the affair." Reaching around Wilson's back, she yanked the gun from his hand.

"So you used me?" Wilson was crying now, and I couldn't help but feel bad for him.

"Just like you used me. So stop your sniveling, Wilson, and man up. This wasn't love. It's just obsession. You're young. Move on with your life."

"Unlike you, Jill, I have a heart. I have feelings. I can't just *move on* like nothing happened." He dropped to his knees, hands reaching for hers.

She backed away from him. "Well, you'd better figure out a way, because I don't ever want to see you again. Stay away from me. Or else."

"Or else what? What will you do if I can't?"

Jill didn't abide threats. And she never negotiated. "Say your goodbyes to your mother while you can." She smirked. "Oh, and here's an idea: give that *fortune* you got for the gun to her. She'll need it when they deport her ass back to Ukraine."

"You cold bitch," Wilson seethed. "This isn't over, Jill. It will never be over!"

But his words couldn't touch her. His anger merely bounced off her retreating back. As Jill stomped past Wilson, kneeling helplessly, her high heels sinking into the soft earth, his eyes followed her. Slipping from his fingers, the letter fell to the ground. And he watched the breeze lift and carry it into the middle of the yard where, later that night, Tony would find it. But the greatest irony was yet to come, for the gun Tony had obtained from the man who was—pardon my language—screwing his wife would be the same gun that killed him six months later.

Chapter 8

THE CAGEY CHEF

August 1982

The ruthless summer heat played cruel tricks on us all. Tormenting our bodies. Fogging our minds. And simmering a righteous rage in thirteen-year-old Charlotte, whose finger pointed at Mickey Hallorann, personal chef for the Eyler Estate, as she accused him of attempted murder.

One might say the day had started off on a sinister note as morning attacked the Western Pennsylvania town with a near-eighty-degree temperature that kept steadily rising, and humidity that gave Jill's hair an epic case of the frizzies. The suffocating heat ignited an irritation that had already been bubbling. By afternoon, the sun baked the last remnant of the semi-cool morning away, along with all of the house staff's patience. Especially that of chef Mickey Hallorann.

It wasn't that Chef Mickey couldn't handle the heat. He'd been born and raised in New Orleans, Louisiana, a city that gave hell a run for its money as far as hot, humid weather goes. There Chef Mickey had trained in the culinary arts under the undisputed queen of Creole cuisine, at Dooky Chase's Restaurant. Filled with art and fine Cajun fare, in the 1960s the restaurant became a hot spot for prominent civil rights leaders, including Dr. Martin Luther King, Jr., to meet and strategize. The gumbo and fried chicken that drew patrons from across the nation also earned Chef Mickey several offers as executive chef when he and his wife relocated north.

Nor was it that Chef Mickey couldn't handle the kids. He had two kids and a sleepless newborn at home, which might have accounted for the slight forgetfulness that led to the "attempted murder," as Charlotte called it.

Perhaps it was a combination of the two—the heat and the exhaustion—that nearly killed Dustin Eyler.

We all felt the prickliness as the day wore on. My shirt collar and underarms—and places decorum prohibits me from mentioning—were drenched with sweat. Clothes sticking to skin. Dense air stifling our breath. It was grueling work in the hot-box house with not a single breeze of relief. While the mansion had been designed using 1880s state-of-the-art ventilation, which involved specially constructed eaves that released the rising hot air and massive first floor windows that allowed cooler air to flow in, none of this could compete with modern-day central air conditioning…which the Eyler Estate had not yet been updated with. Give me modern technology over old-fashioned architecture any day.

By a ninety-three-degree noon, the tension came to a boil.

In the children's game room, Dustin threw down his controller, already tired of his brand-new ColecoVision game system, supposedly more advanced than his barely used Atari. I couldn't tell the difference, but then again, I wasn't the pre-teen demographic. He joined the girls outside in the backyard pool, where Jennifer whooped with refreshed delight as she played a game of Marco Polo with Charlotte.

Wrapped in towels and dripping wet, the kids slipped into the kitchen demanding chocolate chip pecan cookies—and only freshly baked would do. No fruit salad, or banana pudding, or ice cream, or any other easier, cooler snack offering Chef Mickey suggested would suffice. So against every ounce of self-preservation, Mickey agreed to crank on the oven and bake the cookies—and himself along with them.

Thirty minutes later—and five degrees hotter—the kids ran outside with their cookies, happily coating their fingers in chocolatey goo.

Twenty minutes later Dustin returned, not feeling so well.

Ten minutes after that Charlotte was yelling for her mother as Dustin's face swelled to nearly twice its normal size and he labored to breathe.

Somewhere between then and when the ambulance arrived, Charlotte figured out it was the pecans in the cookies. Dustin was allergic. While he was rushed to the waiting ambulance, with Jill talking over everything the EMT was trying to say, Tony demanded answers.

When Tony threw open the swinging kitchen door, Mickey stood at the center island recounting the events to me while sharpening his knives—or as Mickey called it, "steeling" his knives. I recognized his most commonly used chef's knife that he was currently working on, running the blade up and down the steel sharpening rod. After a few runs of this, he would slide the blade back and forth across the whetstone to finish it up. Mickey was reaching for his paring knife as Tony smacked his hand on the countertop.

"Why were there nuts in those cookies, Mickey?"

Mickey started at his employer's accusation, dropping the paring knife. He could have told the truth—that Charlotte requested them. And Charlotte got what Charlotte wanted, or else they'd be having a similar battle over Chef Mickey not abiding the kids' requests. But as a Black man he also knew better than to blame an entitled white girl. He was damned if he did, damned if he didn't.

"You tried to kill my brother!" Charlotte screamed between sobs while Tony's attention shifted back and forth between his frantic daughter and silent employee. "You've always hated Dustin. You knew what you were doing."

Sweat beaded down Mickey's face as her accusation flew across the kitchen. I wasn't sure if the perspiration was a result of the heat, or the interrogation he was under. He knew without a doubt who the police would side with if this went any further than the kitchen. And we all knew that Tony tended to shoot first and ask questions later.

"Charlotte, you know that's not true," Mickey calmly said. "I never meant to hurt your brother. I had no idea he had eaten one of the cookies."

But Charlotte turned to her father with a severe look of doubt. "He's lying, Dad. You know this was no accident."

"It doesn't matter if you meant to or not, Mickey. It was irresponsible of you. You know Dustin's allergic to nuts, and your negligence could have cost him his life. I'm sorry, but we're going to have to let you go."

"Wait—you're firing me?"

"You gave me no other choice." Tony folded his arms.

Mickey's eyes widened. "Sir, with all due respect, I've never made a mistake in all the years I've been working for you. I'm not the one who buys the groceries for this house, so you can't blame me when your kids choose to eat things they know they're not allowed to have. I'm a professional chef, not a babysitter."

"This was hardly professional what you just did. Consider today your last."

"C'mon, man. I have a wife, two kids, and a newborn at home. You know the job market is terrible right now. And you're going to fire me over one accident?"

"You almost killed my kid!" Tony slammed his fist down again, rattling the set of knives. "I should do a lot more than just fire you for this!" Reaching across the island, Tony grabbed Mickey's collar, pulling his chest closer.

Mickey reflexively slid the handle of the paring knife against his palm. A blank stare was all Mickey needed to cow Tony, who released his grip and stepped back.

Adjusting his shirt collar, Mickey sniffed and remained calm but tactical. "I could understand if Dustin was a little child and I fed it to him. But he's old enough to know what a pecan looks like and to not eat it. He's ten years old. I have a daughter the same age, and she knows what she's allowed and not allowed to do. I feel like you're being a bit harsh on me when your daughter right there specifically asked for pecans in the cookies."

Tony shot a look at Charlotte. "Is this true?"

She shook her head stubbornly. "No, Daddy, I told you. He's lying."

A father can often see the truth through his children's lies, and in this case Tony Eyler detected something was off. Off enough that he retracted his decision.

"I'm going to give you one more chance, Mickey. But if anything like this ever happens again, you're done."

Tony left the kitchen with a sigh, guiding Charlotte ahead of him. I shifted toward Mickey to comfort him, then thought better of it. In his hand was the paring knife, his knuckles pale as he gripped it. Suddenly I felt Mickey would prefer to be alone.

Despite that day's resolution, Tony's grace period wouldn't last long. Within one month Mickey was forced to leave after Charlotte accused him of inappropriately touching her. Within two months the Eylers pressed charges. Within three months, as summer faded to autumn, one man would be fighting to get his life back and the other man would be dead.

Chapter 9

THE MAID WITH A MOTIVE

October 1982

After the national Tylenol scare the week before, the family became suspicious of everyone. Wary of everything. Every medicine bottle had been tossed out, every prescription emptied down the drain. The Eyler kids would most certainly not go trick-or-treating this Halloween. While I doubted whoever laced the Tylenol capsules with potassium cyanide in Chicago, Illinois, was coming for the Eyler family next, the Eylers were right about one thing:

They could trust no one.

Especially not Annette Wilkes, maid, mother of four, and the most recent victim of their malice.

I never could piece together what exactly happened that day as I eavesdropped from the other side of the parlor entry. It should have been a perfect day. The weather was an ideal mix of fresh nippiness warmed by a generous sun. The air was saturated with the earthy scent of mounds of marigold-yellow leaves, decaying on the wet earth, and the homey fragrances of wood fires and apples ripening on the trees.

Every range of color, from scarlet to ginger to sunflower, clung to tree limbs, their short life hanging on the whim of a strong breeze. As I said, it was a perfect day…until it wasn't.

It started with a cross, and ended in death.

The credenza glistened beneath a polish of lemony wax. The Victorian parlor chairs were dusted and vacuumed to perfection. The antique floral rug was swept, and the tall, spotless windows smelled of ammonia.

With her dull brown hair pulled into a wispy bun, Annette scrubbed and polished, swept and wiped, until the parlor was pristine. There was nary a crumb to reveal that a family of five—three of which were messy children—lived here. That is how well Annette did her job.

She had just finished up for the day and was collecting her supplies to return to the closet under the main stairwell. The sun hung low, casting an orange glow throughout the parlor, which Jill was passing through on the way to the kitchen.

"Goodnight, ma'am," Annette chirped as they passed in opposite directions.

"Derl will have tomorrow's to-do list waiting for you in his office," Jill said without looking at her. "Hold on!" She stopped Annette with a tight grip on her forearm.

"Where did you get that necklace?"

Jill had never engaged her in conversation, so Annette was more than a little surprised. First she set down her dusting supplies and wiped her hands down the skirt of her brown wool dress. Then she fingered the gold chain that rested atop her olive turtleneck, gently holding the necklace out for Jill's inspection.

"Oh, this? This is my mother's. With everything going on with her health issues, she wanted to make sure she gave it to me personally before...anything happened."

Tears soaked her dull brown eyes as she said this, and I felt my own insides knotting with emotion. Annette had already lost a father and faced the grim prospect of her mother not making it to the end of the year.

Jill seemed unfazed by Annette's suffering as she set her jaw. "You're sure that belonged to your mother? Because it looks an awful lot like mine."

Before I continue, it's important to note that I'll always side with Annette's version of the story. She was no thief, no matter how desperate her family had become after the double-dip recession peaked in July of 1981. And the cross necklace clinging to her neck, resting on her collarbone, had indeed been her mother's. But when Jill spotted it and thought it looked like her very own gold cross necklace and accused Annette of stealing it, there was no way to prove who it belonged to. It was one person's word against another, and we all knew who held the upper hand here.

"I assure you, ma'am," Annette insisted, "this is absolutely my mother's. She gave it to me last weekend."

Jill fondled the cross with her usual avarice. "How coincidental that last weekend is when my own necklace went missing."

It was a she said/she said battle of wills. Who would cave? There was only one person who couldn't afford to fight back, and it wasn't Jill.

"I don't know how else to prove to you that this is my mother's, Mrs. Eyler."

Jill released the cross and folded her arms tightly. "Well, then I guess if you're willing to put your job at risk to keep the necklace, that's fine. Keep the jewelry, and you can finish out the day here and I'll get your last paycheck ready."

It was hardball Jill was playing, and Annette didn't even have a bat.

"You know I can't afford to lose this job. I have four kids, and my husband is still out of work after the steel company let him go. Please, I will help you find the necklace you're missing if you'll just give me a chance."

Jill puckered her lips as if considering this very reasonable request. "Nope. Sorry, Annette. I can't trust that you're not stealing from me. You know how the world is now—trust no one. If you can't trust *medicine,* of all things, to be safe, who can you trust?"

"But Miss Jill, you *know* me! I would never do

anything to jeopardize this job."

"I'm sorry, but people are evil. That includes you. So, the choice is yours. Give me the necklace and keep your job, or let yourself out."

"That is completely unfair, ma'am. I've been loyal to you for years. Why would you think you can't trust me now suddenly?"

Jill clucked. "You heard what some crazy person did, putting poison in Tylenol bottles! This world has gone nuts. And now I see you wearing my necklace…it makes me think maybe you're not so innocent after all."

Annette had only one choice. Her family's survival meant more than a piece of jewelry, no matter how sentimental that cross was to her. As she unclasped it from her neck and handed it over, upstairs in her bedroom little Jennifer clasped a very similar cross necklace around the plastic neck of her Cabbage Patch doll, which Jill would discover later that night but fail to mention to anyone.

Jill walked away wearing Annette's necklace, while Annette walked away vowing under her breath that one day the Eylers would get their just deserts. Jill must have overheard it, because she paused at the parlor doorway, slowly turned, and shot Annette a scathing look. "What did you say?"

The words poured out before Annette could stop them. "I was just quoting Scripture from Leviticus 24:19–22."

"Oh?" Jill's red eyebrow tilted, creating a wave of wrinkles across her forehead. "And what does Leviticus have to say?"

Annette paused. I mentally begged her to silence, but her hurt drowned out any logic or self-preservation. *"And whoever causes an injury to a neighbor must receive the same kind of injury in return: Broken bone for broken bone, eye for eye, tooth for tooth. Anyone who injures another person must be injured in the same way in return."*

Jill's jaw dropped. "Are you saying you're going to try to get revenge on me for taking *my* necklace back?"

Thankfully Annette took a long moment to think before she replied. "No, ma'am. It's just today's Bible verse from my devotional."

The lie seemed to satisfy Jill, for Annette didn't lose her job that day. But one week later Jill announced that due to budget cuts, she'd be letting her go. Two weeks later, when Annette showed up on the Eyler Estate doorstep begging for her job back, a new maid answered the door. Three weeks later Annette's family was evicted from their apartment when their monthly rent doubled and they could no longer afford it. Four weeks later her husband took his own life after a terrible fight over the endless cycle of debt the couple was drowning in.

As I said, it started with a cross and ended with Annette's husband's death. And shortly after that, the entire Eyler family ended up dead too.

Part 4

Derl Newman: "Based on what I've told you, as you can see, there are five different people with five different motives to hate—and even kill—the Eyler family. So it wasn't an easy case for the police to crack. In fact, it was downright impossible, since all of the suspects had access to the library, fingerprints all over the house, and a reason to want the Eylers dead. And yet everyone also had an alibi for the night of the murder."

Keisha Fenty: "It's been forty years with no answers, and I think we've waited long enough to find out the truth, Derl. Tell us what we've been dying to know: who killed the Eyler family, and why?"

Chapter 10

THE LONE WITNESS

November 1982

One witness told me everything I needed to know. An unlikely witness. A witness no one gave a second thought to, except for me. Because on the night I found the Eyler family dead, I brought that witness home with me. And one look told me that everything I thought I knew was wrong.

All the clues had been laid out before me in the grisly scene I walked in on that awful Monday. The gunshots to the chest. The bodies arranged in a pentagram. The eyes gouged out by a knife. The books on the faces. The message of revenge. It was as if each suspect played a different part in executing the perfect, well, *execution.*

I thought about the butler, Martin. His Swiss Army knife held immense sentimental value, and he kept it on him at all times. It was the perfect size for gouging out their eyes, and after losing his mother's photos along with his job in a single day, I could imagine him brooding with rage. But the biggest clue was stamped on his skin. As soon as I saw the pentagram tattoo on his arm, it connected too coincidentally with the pentagram shape that the family had been arranged in. Martin told the detectives he'd spent that night at home watching the popular nighttime soap opera *Dallas*, an alibi confirmed by his roommate. When pressed, Martin had recounted the episode in great detail, thus allaying not only the detectives' suspicions, but my own as well.

Then I considered the mailman, Wilson. Jill Eyler's secret lover turned bitter enemy. The family had been shot with the very gun he had sold her cuckolded husband. The ballistics report verified the weapon as a 9mm…which fit the caliber of the Walther PPK. Could it be mere happenstance that Wilson was the only one, besides Tony Eyler, who knew how to load the notoriously temperamental weapon—then expertly hit his mark not one, not two, but five times with a lethal shot? The mother he lived with of course provided his alibi, explaining that he had been home helping her cook authentic chicken Kiev and *borscht*. Her explanation, along with the *deruny* potato pancakes that she fed the investigators, seemed to sufficiently satisfy their questions…along with their stomachs.

Next was Chef Mickey. Though the unlikeliest of the bunch to commit murder, don't forget the man was severely sleep deprived, with a newborn baby at home. It's conceivable that, in this impaired condition, he could have sleepwalked his way through murder. Not to mention, he was a master with a blade. I saw the way he held that paring knife in white-knuckled raged as Mr. Eyler reprimanded him. While anyone could potentially aim a gun and shoot it, only Chef Mickey, among the suspects, seemed capable of wielding a knife the way the killer did, with almost surgical precision. Yet he'd been down at the police station defending his innocence against Charlotte's allegations the night of the murder.

The maid Annette was next on my list. After so much loss because of the Eylers—her job, her home, then her husband—I couldn't imagine a more likely motive for murder. The removal of the eye from the victim lined up a little too closely with her last words to Mrs. Eyler: "An eye for an eye."

Lastly was the gardener, Carrie. The Eylers had broken her spirit, taunted her daughter, humiliated her on a daily basis. The tipping point? I imagine it was when Tony Tyler casually crushed her aspiration to become a writer like a bug under his heel. The books laid out across each face sent a message that only one who understood the power of the written word could deliver: a writer.

Each individual added another piece of the puzzle that almost fit. Almost. But the witness gave me the final clue to reveal the full picture. A picture I wished I had never seen.

I should not have been there that Monday morning. As I mentioned previously, my mother had just passed away, and all I wanted to do was hide. Grieve. Cling to my memories and wallow in the pain. But when you're an estate manager in charge of a sprawling house with countless moving parts, one can't afford the luxury of grief. So I pushed my sadness deeper inside and buried myself in work.

When I had walked into the house that Monday morning, the first thing I noticed was the vase of bloodred roses still sitting in the entryway, cut and arranged on Thanksgiving Day, hours before the party that the Eylers hosted for all their closest colleagues and kin. The blooms were an unexpected treat during an unseasonably warm Indian summer, which was bullied away by a freak snowstorm Thanksgiving night. This reminded me to check with Carrie about some tulip bulbs that were to be delivered later that afternoon. I found her out by the garden shed, pruning shears in hand, happily cutting the deadwood out of a lilac bush. I noticed fresh scratches on her hands—just like the ones Styx gave her when she tried to shoo or pet him.

We exchanged pleasant good mornings and chatted about the weather, the holiday weekend. She asked about my mother, whom she knew was ill. I barely got the words out—*"she passed away on Thanksgiving"*—before breaking down in Carrie's arms. She held me with a warmth and tenderness I hadn't felt in years. She excused herself, then returned several minutes later with her purse, which she had retrieved from her car. She took out a chapbook containing Emily Dickinson's poem "The

Bustle in a House." A spare poem about the effects of death on a household:

> The Bustle in a House
>
> The Morning after Death
>
> Is solemnest of industries
>
> Enacted upon Earth –
>
> The Sweeping up the Heart
>
> And putting Love away
>
> We shall not want to use again
>
> Until Eternity –

"I want you to have this." She handed me the tiny hardbound book, worn from hands that had reached for it far too often. "The words got me through the loss of my own parents long ago. I think it may offer you some comfort."

"Thank you, Carrie. This means a lot to me."

We hugged again, and her warmth radiated through my leather coat, a cheap imitation of the one worn by Hutch in *Starsky & Hutch*. When she released me, resting her palm on my cheek, something felt different about her. Her demeanor. She looked radiant, weightless. As if her whole soul-crushing past had been erased and a new, confident version of her had emerged.

I didn't think much of it until later, when I headed inside the house. After finding it strangely empty, I eventually made my way to the library and found Styx chowing down on the family.

Styx, the lone witness. The one whose claws matched the marks on Carrie's hands. This small but significant detail told me that Carrie had indeed been in this very room, with this very cat, very recently.

The minutiae didn't congeal into a fully-formed suspicion until much later as I imagined her broken heart prodding her to go upstairs, past the bedrooms, up another flight of stairs, until she reached the uppermost landing. Hopelessness would have forced her steps toward the closed library door, and upon entering, the family may not have noticed her opening up the glass case where the Walther PPK was kept. It was already loaded back when Jill first fired it months prior, with seven rounds left. By the time anyone detected her, Carrie could have gotten at least two shots off, one for Tony and one for Jill. The children I imagine she would have had a harder time with…until memories of how they tormented her own precious daughter—their mocking *Shmelly* echoing in her head—gave her the push she needed to tighten her finger around the trigger one, two, three more times.

As the moon bathed the massive bookcases in milky white, I could imagine Carrie glancing out the window, wishing upon a star that it had never come to this. If only Tony had given her book a chance, if only Jennifer hadn't destroyed Martin's photo album, if only Jill hadn't toyed with Wilson's heart, if only Charlotte had treated Chef Mickey with the respect he deserved, if only Jill hadn't taken Annette's precious necklace…if only, if only…

Thus it wasn't a pentagram that the bodies were arranged in. It was the North Star, the symbol of hope that the Eylers had taken from her.

And it wasn't a Swiss Army pocket knife or paring knife that gouged their eyes out. It was Carrie's pruning shears, always on her person, always trimming away the bad that choked out the good.

Lastly, it was not the biblical eye for eye that Carrie sought justice for as she removed each eyeball. In a much simpler sense, the act reflected Cassiopeia looking down on them with an ever-watchful warning gaze as she judged their egotism. One eye for the butler. One for the mailman. One for the chef. One for the maid. And one final eye for herself.

I imagined the placement of a book upon each face was her way of apologizing, as it were, for the fact it had to come to this. The books were a parting gift—a story that would travel with them into the afterlife.

Being the sensitive soul that she was, Carrie would have noticed the cat and tried to pick him up so he would not end up locked in the library after she left for the weekend. But as Styx always did, he had scratched her hand and fled, leaving the only evidence that would point to Carrie as killer. In a way it was fitting, for it was a time-tested literary trope: the writer gone mad.

Chapter 11

The Smoking Gun

Now

As I poured my final revelation into Keisha's ears, I watched her expression change. A slight shift from attentive listener to serious doubter.

"I can see you don't believe me. Just like the police."

Her dazzling teeth were the perfect contrast to her caramel lipstick. A lovely color on her "Is my doubt that evident?"

"What doesn't fit? I've gone through it in my head a million times. Certainly I can't be wrong on this. I was always there. I saw everything. I heard everything."

Tapping a polished fingernail on her chin, Keisha lifted her gaze to study the cathedral ceiling for a moment, then looked back at me. "I've been in this game for a while now. You have to admit, Derl, your interpretation of the massacre is pretty far-fetched."

The cameraman glanced up at me, his mouth smeared with the Butterfinger he was inhaling. "She's right, dude," he said, dropping crumbs on the camera. "No offense."

I squirmed uncomfortably in my chair, resisting the urge to tell this Neanderthal to mind his own business.

"Aren't most murders pretty far-fetched?" I lifted my arm, the movement sending a jolt of pain through my body. Wincing, I realized I was long overdue for my painkillers. "Consider Harvey Richardson, a retired librarian killer. Or Catherine Kett, who killed her daughter because she had stayed out too late with her boyfriend. Or Geraldine Kelley, who stuffed her husband in a freezer. Normal everyday people do far-fetched things, Keisha."

"I get it, but it's hard to align such a violent crime, especially against children, with such a kind woman— and a mother herself. I'm not saying it doesn't happen, but..."

"She was humiliated by Mr. Eyler, and his kids taunted her daughter. If anyone was most likely to snap after all she'd been through, it was Carrie."

Was it so shocking that a person could kill a whole family in cold blood? After all, we are all capable of hate. Our blood runs black with it. Hatred crosses political parties, genders, religions. It seeps into the ideologies of race, sexuality, class. It's everywhere, at all times, festering, bubbling over.

With the right trigger from the wrong person, it was only a matter of time before hatred spilled over into murder. In my opinion, Keisha Fenty knew nothing about the *real* human condition.

"I'm just not buying it, Derl. While she was the only one without an alibi, I can't interview her because she's dead. Without being able to verify with her what you've told me, I find your guesswork...flimsy."

Over the years I had tried to keep in touch with the staff as best I could, until one by one they passed on. First Carrie died back in November of 1992, a decade to the day of the murder. The early 2000s took first Wilson, then Mickey. Martin was miraculously still alive in a nursing home at just shy of 100 years old, in the final stage of dementia—a living death, you might say. Only Annette and I were left among the living, but after the murder she had wanted nothing to do with me.

I huffed. "I wouldn't say my guesswork was *flimsy*. Carrie died on the ten-year anniversary of the murder. Don't you think that's a sign of guilt?"

"Perhaps...perhaps not. That could just be coincidental. But if indeed she took her life out of guilt for her crimes, why no deathbed confession?"

"Okay, so tell me—who do *you* think did it, if not Carrie? Considering you can't interview any of the other suspects..."

Keisha smirked. "I'm still working through that."

"I'm telling you, Keisha, Carrie is the only person who could have done it."

"Except you're wrong about something."

"What's that?"

"You mentioned she was in good spirits when you saw her the Monday after the murder, correct?"

I vividly recalled Carrie's empathetic smile. Her warmth as she hugged me. Her kindness as she handed me the Emily Dickinson book. I felt terrible attaching the crime to her, but there was no one else to blame. When I heard she had died on the anniversary of the murder, it raised a lot of questions in me, one in particular: Could it have been her who did it? That was the moment I knew.

"Yes, she was definitely in good spirits. I'm assuming because she had finally gotten the revenge she always wanted."

"Did you know that she sold her manuscript earlier that week? For quite a nice sum of money, too."

"She did? Why didn't she say anything to me about it?"

"It was Thanksgiving week, so I'm guessing everyone was busy. Then you had just lost your mother. She probably thought it would be crass to mention it, with you grieving. I'm sure she would have told you eventually...if things hadn't happened the way they did. Considering all she had to gain with the book deal, I doubt she would have risked losing it."

It felt like a stab of betrayal that Carrie had never told me during that last week we had worked together.

"Can you say with full certainty that you ruled out Martin Poe, Wilson Farmiga, Mickey Halloran, and—" Keisha rifled through her notes, at a loss for the maid's name.

"Annette Wilkes," I supplied.

"That's right." Her fingernail underscored the name she'd written earlier in her notebook. "Annette Wilkes. Now *she* is someone I'd like to discuss in more detail. I had a chance to speak with her a few weeks ago."

"You interviewed Annette? Why didn't…anyone tell me?"

"I didn't want you to know. And I wouldn't call it an interview. Nothing like this. Just an informal chat."

"And?" I pressed.

"She told me her father was a World War II veteran and her mother was a nurse. She came from a family of heroes."

"Yes, I'm aware." I wasn't sure where she was going with this, but I didn't like it.

"Apparently you two were pretty close, up until the murder happened. She said you had a falling out after that."

"It was pretty traumatic for everyone. It's understandable that she didn't want to keep in touch."

Keisha leaned forward, patting the crime scene photo that still rested on her lap. "Especially if she was trying to hide something."

"What are you getting at, Keisha?"

She cocked her head, her stare penetrating me. "I think we both know it was Annette, Derl. And for some reason you're covering for her."

I stopped her train of thought with a shake of my head. "There's no way it was Annette. No possible way. And I have no reason to cover for her. You've got it wrong…" Slapping my palms on my thighs, I rose with a pained grunt. "And I've got to get going."

"Why are you protecting her?" Keisha's eyes remained locked on mine, pleading.

"Look, I told you everything I know, but it's getting late and I should be heading home." I flashed the face of my watch at her. "Time for my meds."

Keisha rose with me, signaling something to the cameraman. "It's a shame we couldn't resolve the case, but I appreciate you meeting with me. I must say, it's a fascinating story. And almost convincing. Except for one thing you missed."

"I didn't miss anything, Miss Fenty."

Her eyebrow arched. "You said that Carrie had cat scratches on her hands—and that was the main thing that pointed to her being the killer. But you didn't mention seeing any allergic reaction or rash on her that Monday. In fact, I believe you said she looked '*radiant*.'"

My brain fumbled for an explanation. I didn't have one, other than the simplest one. "If she had an allergic reaction, it could have healed over the weekend, I suppose. But if the scratches didn't come from the cat, then how do you explain all the cuts on her hands?"

Keisha latched on to this idea with a full bite. "You told me that she had been cutting roses the day before the murder, and she'd been removing deadwood that Monday morning. Those scratches could have been from that."

"All true. That still doesn't mean she didn't do it." I took a step toward the door, eager to end this conversation. "Well, sorry I don't have anything else to offer. I had hoped to close the case for everyone, but maybe I was wrong about everything. I had really thought I nailed it."

Keisha followed me through the library, past the wall-mounted case where the Walther PPK sat behind a pane of dusty glass. I paused barely a heartbeat to glance at the gun that had taken so many lives.

"Derl, just one more question. Please." Keisha's voice was soothing and gentle, luring me to listen. "Don't you find it strange that they never recovered the gun that fired the shots that night?"

Now I could see what made Keisha so good at her job. She was relentless.

I shot her a curious look. "What do you mean? The police told me it was a German 9mm. I thought it was this gun." I pointed at the locked wooden display holding the Walther PPK.

"You think they would leave the murder weapon here, in this display case, instead of taking it in as evidence? Don't be ridiculous, Derl."

"I...I...don't understand..." How had I missed that? I should have caught that, but I hadn't returned here since the discovery. "The police report said it was a German

9mm."

"That's correct, but it was actually a German *Luger* 9mm, the kind of gun Annette's father brought home from World War II."

"What makes you think Annette had a German Luger?"

"Because she told me, Derl. She told me all about the gun, how her father taught her to shoot with it, how she sold it to Tony years before the murder to help pay for her sick mother's hospital bills. Remember, Tony was a gun collector. It all fits, Derl. Annette knew where the gun was kept, how to load and fire it, how to hit her target. She had reason to hate the Eylers after all she'd lost because of them—her job, her home, her husband. What I can't figure out, though, is why you're protecting her."

The whole gamut of emotions flooded me all at once. The rage at the injustice. The pain of loss. The heartbreak of watching the people I loved crushed at the hands of a heartless monster.

"I'm protecting her because no one else would!"

Chapter 12

Now

I loathed the look Keisha judged me with. A pitying gaze. An accusing stare.

"What do you mean, no one else would protect her?" Keisha asked.

"You're right that Annette had every motive in the world to want that family dead. And no one seemed to care about what they had done to her. Except for me."

"Is it because you understood her loss?"

"What do you mean?"

"You both lost a mother that week, didn't you?"

A potent vision of my dying mother seized my mind. I didn't want to answer Keisha's question; my entire body revolted against it. My tongue felt as dry and rough as sandpaper. My legs felt heavy like weights. Yet even if I could run, there was nowhere for me to go.

I glanced back to find the cameraman still filming. Keisha knew. It was far too easy for Keisha to fact-check any lie I gave her. In fact, I could see I had underestimated Keisha Fenty. It appeared she had already known about my omission and set me up. This whole thing was a devious ploy just to get my confession on record.

"I know the truth, Derl. You protected Annette because you both share the same mother, and you both shared the pain of her death. Annette Wilkes is your sister, isn't she?" Keisha wasn't asking because she already knew the answer.

While I tended to the Eyler Estate on Thanksgiving night while the family hosted a party to end all parties, Annette sat at our mother's bedside watching her die. And I wasn't there for either of them.

"Yes, you're correct. She's my sister."

"I remember discovering that little nugget during my research on the case. You got her the job too, didn't you?"

I nodded. "I did. So now you're looking into me, Miss Fenty?" Suddenly our first-name basis felt too familiar, too casual. There was no crime in my family history, so why did I feel like our interview was suddenly turning into an interrogation?

She chuckled. "Of course. It's my job to look at every person involved as a suspect, at every angle. Including you."

I could see the wheels cranking inside that pretty head of hers. Somewhere along this interview I had said too much.

"I don't blame you, Derl, for wanting to protect your sister. But I do blame you for not being fully honest with me."

"I apologize for my lack of transparency, but I don't want my sister to go to jail."

"You don't have to worry about that. She's not going to jail. But I'm not talking about how you kept your relationship to Annette a secret. I'm talking about *you*."

"Me?"

Keisha handed me the crime scene photo she'd shown me at the start of our interview, depicting Tony's dead body in graphic detail. I stifled a shudder.

She tapped a fingernail against the photo, near Derl's neck. "Do you notice something unusual about this picture?"

"More unusual than a man with a hole in his chest and a hole in his eye socket?"

"I didn't notice it at first either. But the moment I walked into this room and saw you, it all clicked."

"What do you mean?" Though I was afraid to ask.

"When I first started pulling all the files on this case, I noticed Tony's tie. Something about it nagged at me. There were too many controversies over blood spatter analysis to assume it had been tied postmortem. But that knot—I had never seen one done like that."

"You mean a café knot?"

"Exactly—the stylish but absurdly complicated café knot, one of the more difficult knots to learn. And especially hard to do on a dead body. Only someone of your sartorial elegance would know how to tie a café knot, someone who just so happens to be wearing the same exact same knot as we speak."

My hand instinctively rose to my neck, pointlessly hiding my tie. "What are you getting at, Miss Fenty?"

"I think you know, Mr. Newman."

I couldn't help but chuckle that something as simple as how I tie my tie would be my downfall.

You see, it wasn't a Walther PPK that was used to kill each member of the Eyler family. Rather, it was my father's very own German Luger, passed down along with his Constellation watch, which was inscribed on the back with the words:

Time heals all wounds.

And yet living and working with the Eyler family showed me the deep flaws in my father's core belief. Time didn't heal all wounds. Instead it made them fester. Each day the Eylers stole hope, dashed dreams, thieved joy, and crushed souls, the infection grew.

Even now, with my greatest secret poised to be revealed on a national scale, I had no regrets. Closing my eyes, my memory took me back to that moment. As my finger tightened around the trigger, I was one squeeze away from taking back all the power that had been stolen from me. Another pull gave the butler his dignity. Another flinch restored the gardener's hope. Another jerk gave the mailman his freedom. And one last twitch gave my sister her life back. At least that was how I viewed it in the moment, no matter how much a monster the media was sure to paint me as.

Keisha knew she had me, but she could never understand why. Not unless you knew the Eylers. As my mother lay dying, gasping for her final breath alone while my boss forbade me from leaving to be at her bedside that Thanksgiving evening, I missed her final moments. I missed a last goodbye. I lost a chance to touch her warm skin before it grew cold and rigid in death. It was a loss that would leave an everlasting ache within me.

After Carrie had died, she seemed the most reasonable and fitting choice to blame. It protected me and my sister. No harm, no foul. But it was the Eylers who created the perfect murder. A family of villains. A house of suspects. A slew of motives. I could take any pick and draw a logical conclusion. But I had never anticipated it would circle back to me.

"Which begs the question, Derl." Keisha examined my face as she spoke. "Why the whole gruesome display?"

"To be honest, I had compiled a series of murder scenes from various crime shows. Then I worked in details that I noticed about the staff. It may look like I was overdoing it, but I needed something that would throw the police off, and it seemed to work."

"That takes a special kind of...sociopathy to pull that off, Derl."

"That could explain why I'm still single."

Keisha didn't laugh. Instead she bulldozed forward. "Why did you fix Tony's tie after you killed him?"

I had never considered the why of that small—yet ultimately damning—act. "Despite what I had done to them, I did take care of them. I had worked for them for a decade, tending to their every need. I guess it was instinct kicking in to manage that last little detail. I wanted Tony to look good before I let him rot in hell."

Keisha nodded as if she understood.

"So I guess I'm going to jail, huh?"

Keisha glanced at the cameraman, then back at me. In her eyes I saw understanding. She'd met people like the Eylers. And she'd met killers like me. As our gazes locked, I didn't know how my story would end, if Keisha would turn me in or let me go. But I would accept my fate, because in the end, we all get what we deserve.

"It is terminal?" she asked.

"What—my cancer? How did you know?"

"Annette may have mentioned it. Along with your sleeplessness, hallucinations, and paranoia."

"For someone who wants nothing to do with me, my sister sure seems to involve herself in my business. But yes, the doctor gives me another four months or so, if I'm lucky."

Keisha placed a hand on my shoulder. "You know, I found it ironic that the three murderers you mentioned earlier—Harvey Richardson, Catherine Kett, and

Geraldine Kelley—all made deathbed confessions. Is that what this is, Derl?"

I began to grow tired of this dance. Of this whole damn life. "I don't know. I guess that depends on if you're going to turn me in."

Keisha thought before answering. "The documentary won't air for at least a year—long after you're gone. This case has gone unsolved for almost forty years. What's another couple months?"

I couldn't believe what I was hearing. "Are you letting me go?"

"At this point, what's the purpose of serving a couple months in jail? You and everyone you cared about suffered enough, Derl. This is your free pass to make amends before you die. Reconcile with your sister. Take that exotic trip your mom wanted for you. The police will have its closure on this case once you're gone. Deal?"

I couldn't find the words to thank Keisha Fenty, but I felt every bit of gratitude. And hope that maybe the world wasn't so evil after all. And a dash of joy that I could live out the rest of my days with my sister. We'd take that trip somewhere warm and exotic like I'd promised my mother. I pulled Keisha into a grateful hug, letting my tears soak the shoulder of her mustard blouse, and she hugged me back.

My father had been right all along. Time *could* heal all wounds. Because for the first time since 1982, my spiraling mind, my haunting guilt, the vengeful ghosts, my festering wounds finally felt vanquished.

THE END…OR IS IT?

**

If you haven't read *A Slow Ruin*, the novel that this story is based on, grab it at your favorite retailer, or at my website at www.pamelacrane.com.

About the Author

PAMELA CRANE is a *USA Today* bestselling author and professional juggler of four kids, a writing addiction, and a horse rescuer. She lives on the edge and writes on the edge...where her sanity resides. Her thrillers unravel flawed women with a villainous side, which makes them interesting...and perfect for doing crazy things worth writing about. When she's not cleaning horse stalls or cleaning up after her kids, she's plotting her next murder.

Join her newsletter to get a FREE book and updates about her new releases and deals at www.pamelacrane.com.

Enjoy what you read?

Then check out LITTLE DOES SHE KNOW, an "addictive psychological thriller!"

A missing boy. A dead body. Four decades apart, but connected by a mysterious link.

It's 1986, the height of big hair, power suits, and "Material Girl." Ginger Mallowan is the epitome of all of these things, until her son disappears during a beach walk one night. That's the moment girls don't want to have fun anymore, and the moment she starts hunting for answers.

It's 2022, and Ginger's hair is a bit flatter, she's retired her power suits, but she still dances to "Material Girl." She hasn't found—or forgotten—her missing son, but she has managed to survive the grief…thanks to her neighbor Tara Christie.

Tara is the friend who keeps Ginger's secrets. But that vow is tested one night when Tara is jarred awake by a scream coming from next-door, where she finds Ginger standing over a dead body. As the investigation shakes the town to its core, and Tara's husband is charged with the murder, Tara must choose between proving her husband's innocence or protecting Ginger's past.

Little does she know she's about to stumble down a twisty path that could destroy them all.

Made in the USA
Monee, IL
03 July 2022

99050178R00073